Pi AGENCY

Neelabh Pratap Singh

First published in 2020 by

Becomeshakespeare.com

Wordit Content Design & Editing Services Pvt Ltd
Unit - 26, Building A -1, Nr Wadala RTO,
Wadala (East), Mumbai 400037, India
T: +91 8080226699

ISBN 978-93-90040-28-5

To all the real-life female detectives
who have transcended the societal norms to become
who they are today

About The Author

Neelabh Pratap Singh is a mechanical engineer by profession. He is an avid reader and a passionate storyteller. He used to fulfil his passion of storytelling in childhood by drawing superhero comic books in his notebooks and colour it with crayons. As he grew up, he started writing short stories on blogs and various online platforms. His passion for storytelling led him to take up the gargantuan task of writing a full-fledged novel. The Resurrection of Evil is his debut novel which is a mythological thriller. He lives in Gurgaon with his wife.

Connect with the author:

Email: neelabhpratap.singh@gmail.com

Facebook: /authorneelabh

Twitter: @authorneelabh

Instagram: @authorneelabh

Acknowledgments

Writing is a solitary job, but transforming an MS word document into a book requires a team effort. I am fortunate that I have been successful in gathering a team which did wonder to my raw manuscript. Here are some of those whom I would like to thank deeply.

My parents, Rakesh and Suhsma, for my constant source of encouragement, My wife, Mohini, for bearing with my absence (sitting idle as a stone in the house while writing is as good as being absent).

Michelle Browne, my editor, who not only polished the language but also gave me valuable suggestions pertaining to plot and characterization.

Vishal Bagaria, for helping me with rewriting the snippets I used to throw at you over FB messenger.

My author friends, Vineet, Sai, and Rohit, for always being ready to offer their valuable inputs.

All those reporters and journalists whose articles have added richness to the plot. Special mention of two famous books – Narconomics: How to run a Drug Cartel by Tom Wainwright and American Kingpin by Nick Bilton, which were my primary source of research.

You, the reader, who have put faith in my book and picked it from the ocean of books available out in the world. Your feedback matters the most.

Lastly, I bow to the almighty for bestowing me with the ability to write this book. I hope I have done justice to the Lord's blessings.

If I have unintendedly missed someone, perhaps we can settle it over a round of drinks.

Prologue

At first, it was red, like the colour of blood. Psychedelic bokeh spots drenched in crimson danced in front of his eyes as Rohan flickered them open. The world was bathed in a deep shade of red. Dull thuds surrounded him and every breath he inhaled took the effort of moving an elephant across a room. The dull thuds morphed into a hum and then into the heavy bass vibration emerging from somewhere to his right. Every beat blasting from the speaker to his right thumped against his ribcage, in sync with his hearbeats. From the corner of his eye, he could discern a discarded syringe lying on the floor by his shoeless feet.

He blinked and tried to make sense of what was happening around him. He felt weightless—as he left the entrapments of gravity far, far behind. Floating like strands of bacteria in naked air. Flying like a bird above a fluffy cloud.

There were movements. Was someone here? He widened his eyes, thinking that it would expand his vision. He noticed the figures moving around him. Black shadowy figures juxtaposed themselves in the red-dyed world around him. Black shadowy figures turned into blonde and wasp-waisted people, their skin flawless and smooth as porcelain, reflecting the encompassing red shade. They were angels – voluptuous and scantily clad. He didn't bother counting their number, for his eyes never left their naked limbs. Their hair cascaded down to their bare breasts. The angels were dancing to the trance music in slow motion. He was now sure that he wasn't on Earth.

But what was this place?

Heaven. Wasn't heaven supposed to be all white?

He tried to move his hands and legs, to float and reach up to the angels. He wanted to appreciate their beauty from a closer look. Feel them with his remaining three senses. But he couldn't move an inch, as if paralysed.

He shuddered. He couldn't feel his limbs. His hands and legs remained unmoved as if he was a corpse. A cadaver bathed in blood.

He squinted and noticed a blurred image of another figure emerging among the angels. Like the angels, this figure, too, had little clothes on its body—naked, in fact. But unlike the angels, its body wasn't reflecting any red hues. It was a perfectly black body—an object which absorbed all the colours of spectrum. He'd studied about it in high school, he guessed.

The angels gave way to the figure—like Red Sea parted for Moses—still dancing, not bothered by the presence of the Black Body. It arrived closer to him. Fear clenched Rohan's heart. It was a Devil.

Rohan was wrong. This wasn't really Heaven. *Blood red... infernal spirits swaying to goth trance... the Devil walking amongst his minions...* It was Hell.

The angels slowly faded away in the background, while the devil inched closer and closer to him.

Chapter 1

Brajesh Arya, owner of a management consulting firm in Gurgaon, stared at the wall thoughtfully. He was sitting inside the office of a drug rehab counsellor. The female counsellor sat across the table. The sun outside shone dangerously, the heat soaring by the minute, and despite being dressed in his impeccable formal suit, as always, he shuddered. His eyes scanned the temperature on the air conditioner – 16 degrees. He shook his head unconsciously. Had it been his own chamber, only God would help his secretary. The temperature would never fall below 20 in his office.

For the past two years, he'd had to visit this place frequently. Not that he needed any help to leave a drug addiction. He never touched these things. In fact, he never smoked and seldom indulged in drinking. He was here because of his son, Rohan, who was sitting beside him—shoulders down, bleary eyes, and face drained of all the colours and brightness that a kid of twenty-one would have.

Two years ago, Brajesh came to know about his son's drug addiction. Rohan had been into substances for quite some time now. What started as a search for a high beyond alcohol had turned into an inescapable obsession. During the early years of Rohan's college, when his son was only seventeen, Brajesh came to know about his son's addiction. The casual use had become abuse. He had immediately admitted him to a drug rehab. He chose a premium rehab centre which offered air-conditioned rooms like a five start hotel, facilities of gym, and a swimming pool. All this so that his son would never feel that he had been deprived of anything. The rehab successfully cured Rohan's addiction. Rohan's life seemed to be back to normal.

But things hadn't gone as Brajesh thought. Today it was the third time in the past two years he had to bring Rohan back to the rehab. Rohan's studies had been hampered. He wasn't looking to be graduated soon. It was disheartening to see his son unable to fight his obsession.

Brajesh brought his mind back to the present and tried to focus on the words of the female counsellor.

"Rohan, you have been coming here for the past two years," the counsellor said with a soft smile. "Of all patients here, I think you are the best one to know that we can only guide you. It's not we who cures a patient, it's only and only the patient who has to cure himself."

"Why do you think I am not trying?" Rohan snapped.

Brajesh placed his hand over Rohan's. He didn't want Rohan to lose his calm.

"You are trying, Rohan, but you aren't fighting."

"Fighting? Do you even know how these urges feel?" Rohan sounded helpless. "It's not that I don't want to leave drugs. I absolutely hate them. I struggle with these yearnings to touch drugs, yet…yet…" Rohan trailed off.

The counsellor maintained her smile, trying to look normal to Rohan. "I understand, Rohan. But you very well know that we can save you from these drugs only while you are here. When you leave this place, you have to stand against your urges. You have to strengthen your will and believe in yourself. Look at your dad, think about his situation. He, too, is fighting along with you. And I am sure you won't let your father down."

Rohan's head turned toward Brajesh, and his eyes dropped down to the floor. His son was ashamed of himself. His son was helpless.

Rohan turned back to the counsellor. "I think my addiction will end only with my life."

"Rohan!" Brajesh cried. No father ever wanted to hear those words from his child. He was disappointed with his son right from the day he'd found about his addiction, but he had never shown his anger. He wanted his son to face the adversities with courage and defeat his weaknesses. Being a businessman, he'd seen tough times. He had lost his wife when Rohan was only five. His budding firm was on the verge of bankruptcy. He fought with the fate, brought his son up along with taking care of his firm. Today where he was standing wasn't due to some miracle. It was because of the never-say-die attitude. And the last thing he would accept in life was surrender, and he expected the same from his son. "Never ever say that again, *beta.*"

Rohan hugged him. A trickle of tear dropped down from Rohan's eyes to Brijesh's shoulder. "Then what do I do, Papa? I'll be trapped in this hell forever. Even if I want to get out of this, I cannot. You know that. He won't..." Rohan paused. He voice was now a whisper. "He won't ever let me come out this trap ever."

Brajesh offered his son a protective embrace. He knew his son was right. His son was helpless. And so was Brajesh. Alphalion would never let his son come back to the normal life.

Chapter 2

Brajesh was lost in his thoughts, rotating a crystal paperweight on the table, the surface of which was etched—Arya Consultants. The paperweight would sparkle with the brilliance of a diamond before, but today, it looked nothing but a cheap counterfeit. For more than an hour, he'd been doing the same thing. Arya Consultants—his management consultancy firm— had a corporate office in Cyber city, Gurgaon. A tower covered with a glass façade all around, it was mere a couple of hundred meters from the national highway. Initially he'd rented a floor for his office, but with time, he acquired the entire building.

Although he owned the company, on paper and literally, he just wouldn't sit in his cabin. It wasn't him. Instead, as soon as his clock instructed, he would step outside his box, run an eye along the bigger box where his employees – his 'men' (irrespective of the gender) – sat, fighting through another day, pick someone without preamble, and have a conversation with the poor sod. Senior management wasn't his cup of tea. Long meetings were sheer wastage of time. Besides, if senior management couldn't handle their own shit, who could? It was the men on the lower rungs who needed his guidance. Once, he plopped himself beside an executive's swivel chair and helped him through the night in completing a client's presentation. But things had changed between then and now. He couldn't focus much on his company's work these days; his mojo was slipping away. And his employees must have been noticed that, too.

He heard a knock at the door.

"May I come in, sir?" It was his secretary, Pooja Sharma.

He nodded.

"Sir, VC with Crystal healthcare is at two."

Brajesh acknowledged, still spinning the paperweight.

"And sir, we haven't submitted this month's report to JC Composites."

Brajesh nodded again. "I will look into it. Anything else?"

The secretary paused for a while and said, "Why don't you speak to the police, sir?"

Brajesh raised his eyes from the paperweight to his secretary. Pooja's expression reflected concerns for her boss. She was aware of Rohan's problem. It was actually his fault. She was the only female in his life who was close to him. Not in any romantic way, but being a secretary, she would remain around him for most of the time, be it in the office or a business trip. They would often go for casual dinners and discuss life outside of the office. He knew about her gay father, or the money-digging ex-boyfriend. She knew a bit lesser about him. But she knew about his son. "I have been to them many times," Brajesh said with a sigh of surrender.

Though he had never been to the police. The kind of problem his son was into, he couldn't afford the news to get out. In the age of social media, there was nothing called privacy. But he knew of another fact – drugs didn't top the priority list of police, instead, it was terrorism. In addition, the police weren't very confident about seeking out the root of the problem. Many policemen were poorly-versed with antinarcotics laws.

Yet police weren't completely at fault. There had been some instances when the policemen had been questioned by the National Drugs and Psychotropic Substances Act for the seizures and arrests, leaving the policemen avoid cases related to drugs.

He stood and walked behind his chair. "I have lost all hope in them. In fact, I have lost all hope in everyone."

He gazed out of the large glass window toward National Highway 48, or NH 8, as the locals would call it by its former name, which connected the capital to major Indian cities like Jaipur, Mumbai, and Chennai. "Is there any man in the city who can help me?"

"There is one," Pooja said.

Brajesh turned around, his brows furrowed in curiosity.

Pooja moved closer to his table and hesitantly placed a business card on it. "Actually…there is a woman."

Brajesh looked down at the business card. It read 'Pi Agency.'

Chapter 3

Akshay was about to put the golgappa in his mouth when he heard his colleague, Diksha, trying to speak while munching the golgappa. "Hold your horses," he said.

"Mmm… it's so delicious. Nothing beats a golgappa," Diksha said, still chomping. Her *golgappa*-filled mouth made her oval face completely round. Wind messed up with her bangs over hear forehead. With her both hands wet with spicy flavoured water, she jerked her head back to clear her forehead of her bangs.

Golgappa—a crispy, hollow rice ball filled with tamarind sauce, spices, mashed potatoes, chickpeas, and yogurt—was a popular Indian street snack, Different regions of India called it by different names – *Panipuri, Paani ke Patashe, Gupchup, fulki.*

"It has a lot of sodium," Akshay said.

Diksha scrunched her brows, still with a mouthful of the water ball.

"High in salt and spices," Akshay explained. "It's going to retain a lot of water in my body." He placed his hand on his belly. "I feel bloated already."

"Oh, shut up, you calorie-conscious gym rat. Learn to enjoy the life."

"Your golgappas are going to get us killed today. We've been out for half an hour and boss doesn't know."

"Are you Courage?"

"What?"

"Courage the Cowardly Dog. The animated series that used to air on Cartoon Network."

"Huh."

"You've never watched it? Were you born in a gym or what?" She filled her mouth with another waterball. "Just drop a text."

Akshay pulled his mobile out of his pocket. As soon as he unlocked his phone, his left hand moved straight his head. "Bloody hell. Four missed calls from boss."

"You are gone," Diksha managed to say, her mouth full of golgappa again.

Akshay quickly tapped the call button. He heard from the other side first and said, "Boss, we're out having golgappas." He paused again to hear something and said again, "Okay, boss, we will be at the office soon."

"What did she say?" Diksha asked as soon as Akshay hung up the call.

"She was angry." Akshay wiped the sweat from his forehead. "But I don't know why she was panting. And also, I heard stuff dropping on the floor."

"Oops! What did she say when you said we're out for golgappas?" Diksha said.

"Leave it," Akshay said, handing the money to the golgappa vendor.

"*Arey*… tell *na*." She pulled Akshay's t-shirt.

"She said, 'Arora, I want you here in two minutes, or else I will pluck off your golgappas.'"

"I knew it," Diksha said, dissolving into hysterical laughter.

Chapter 4

For the fourth time, Rashmi Purohit called her subordinate, Akshay, but much to her disdain, he didn't pick up the call.

Where the fuck these idiots are? Rashmi thought, throwing the mobile phone on the table. She checked the time on the digital table clock kept to her right. *Bhupender Bhatia will be here any moment.*

A moment later, the rusty iron gate outside creaked. She quickly glanced at the CCTV monitor. A grainy image of a burly figure appeared on the screen. *Bhatia is here.*

A few weeks ago, a girl named Priya had hired Rashmi to inquire about her boyfriend, with whom she was planning to marry. Priya suspected that her boyfriend was involved in an affair. She shared a screenshot of WhatsApp chats sent to her by another girl—her boyfriend's colleague—with whom Priya's boyfriend appeared to be cheating. The chats clearly showed her boyfriend had romantic talks with his colleague, and so Priya sought Rashmi's help to provide evidence to call the marriage off. Rashmi shadowed the guy for a few weeks and concluded the case. Before she contacted Priya, she had dropped a message to the guy's father, Bhupender Bhatia.

Footsteps rang in the narrow staircase that led to the basement where the office was located. A shadow spilled across the landing in front of the door before Bhatia appeared.

Bhatia stormed into the office.

"Ms Purohit, what a pathetic joke is this?" Bhatia said, his right hand stretched forward holding his mobile phone. The mobile phone showed Rashmi's message, which she had sent a few hours ago.

Rashmi observed Bhatia's hand trembling. *He is afraid,* Rashmi thought. "The truth, Mr. Bhatia."

"You think it was I who had planned everything?" Bhatia clenched his teeth, putting his mobile phone back inside his pocket.

Bhatia was a stocky man, height a few inches over six feet. Rashmi noticed his balled fist inside his pocket. He was standing still, his shoulders raised. *Okay, so you want some action.*

Rashmi tied her hair behind her neck into a ponytail. "Apparently, yes. I didn't tell anything to your son or his girlfriend, Priya. I called you here to suggest you to get things sorted between your son and his love, and I will not tell anyone anything."

Bhatia scoffed. "What do you mean you won't tell anyone anything? As if you would be in a position to tell anyone anything."

Bhatia swung his fist.

Rashmi jerked back sharply, escaping the blow. Predictable.

"Long ago," Bhatia growled, "when I was not the head of a transport company, I rumbled with ten men. *Chhori*, you don't stand a chance."

She wasn't quick enough to dodge the second blow and Bhatia's meaty fist dashed on her jaws. It seemed his fist was larger than her entire face.

Her mind blacked out for a moment, and she stumbled back, holding the edge of the table to prevent herself from falling on the floor.

Her phone rang. The name displayed 'Akshay Arora'.

The ringtone distracted Bhatia for a moment, and Rashmi noticed that. She grabbed the table clock and threw it at Bhatia. She tapped on the call accept button on the mobile phone and put it on the loudspeaker. "Arora, where the hell are you guys?"

"Boss, we are out for *golgappas*," Akshay's electronic voice radiated out of the mobile phone's loudspeaker.

Rashmi had deliberately picked the call and put the call on loudspeaker, hoping that it would distract Bhatia, and might discourage him to stop his assault after hearing someone else's voice.

But only the former happened. A table clock wasn't enough to hurt this ogre, let alone stopping him.

Bhatia looked down at the fallen table clock and smirked. "What are you going to do next? Attack me with your lipstick?"

"Arora, I want you here in two minutes," she panted, "or else I'll pluck off your *golgappas.*"

Rashmi picked up her rolling chair and threw it at Bhatia.

Bhatia tried to duck, but the projectile found its mark, hit him on the head.

"Oh, the toy seemed to hit you quite hard."

Bhatia rose, his face dark as the eclipsed sun. He approached Rashmi, swinging his hands aggressively, like a maniac.

Rashmi blocked every blow with her forearms. *Enough of the self-defence.* She lifted her right leg and kicked sharply against the left side of Bhatia's ribcage. Hard and pointed front of her running shoes hit him hard. Bhatia bent down, grunting in pain. Without putting her right leg on to the ground, she repeated the action, but this time, against Bhatia's left thigh. His left leg buckled at his knee, and he collapsed on the floor like a demolished building.

Rashmi caught her breath for a while and watched Bhatia lying crumpled on the floor. "I was just respecting your age, uncle," Rashmi said, smashing the final blow on Bhatia's rotund face.

Chapter 5

Akshay and Diksha entered Pi Agency office located in the basement. Their boss, Rashmi Purohit, had converted the basement of her residence into an office. It was a long hall divided by a wooden shelf. While one part was converted into their office, the other was utilised as a storage space. The office was bland in looks. Cheap dark grey vinyl flooring, whitewashed walls, and an antique air-conditioner which his boss would keep off most of the time to save money on electricity bill. An eight by three feet glass topped table and three mesh back rolling chairs with four wheels for all three employees of Pi Agency. The walls were blank and seemed to be whitewashed in some bygone era. A white board on an easel had all the remaining space available for itself.

"Why rent an over-priced office? I don't want to waste my money," Rashmi had said when he asked if she should consider renting a commercial space. "We live in a digital world. Potential clients can easily approach us through our website and mobile based applications."

Boss was right. Pi Agency was still growing. They did not have a filthy rich clientele. Most of the clients were hard-negotiators.

As Akshay stepped inside, he noticed the digital table clock was lying flat on its face. The rolling chair, too, was lying upside down. He quickly glanced at Diksha, who was following her, and gestured with his chin to speak to their boss.

Diksha slowly approached Rashmi. "Boss, we went out for lunch," Diksha said, making a puppy face.

"My dear, time is money for me," boss said, her fingers tapping the smartphone screen like those of the typists, "and you know well what my stance on money is. So throw your excuses and whatnot in the trash and get back to work."

Diksha nodded. With the same puppy face, she pulled the fallen chair upright and quietly sat on it.

Akshay eyed Diksha, who began to type quickly on her laptop. *Acting if she has a lot of work.* Akshay understood there was no point in adding anything else, for it would only get him to hear some more expletives from his boss. Like Diksha, he chose to sit quietly on a chair, but noticed his chair wasn't around. He scanned the office. When his gaze settled on his chair, he was taken aback. A stocky man with a bruised face and tape wrapped around his mouth was tied to it. The chair looked tiny against his size.

He glanced at Diksha, who was equally amused by the sight. They both looked at Rashmi.

"You remember that girl's case who had hired us to find if her boyfriend was cheating on him?" Rashmi said. "He is the guy's father."

"When did he come into the picture?" Akshay asked.

"He was always in the picture," Rashmi said.

Akshay looked at Diksha. She only shrugged.

Rashmi put her phone on the table and began. "So, you two followed and observed that guy, but didn't find anything suspicious. Then I started working as a full-time maid at the guy's house..." Bhatia's muffled voice interrupted her. "I think he is wondering why he didn't recognize me when he walked down today at our office." Rashmi winked. "So, where was I? Yes— so of course, I noticed the guy's habits, such as with whom he talks, but my prime motive was to frequently check out his mobile phone whenever I found the right time. The guy was in contact with his colleague, the girl with whom he was allegedly having an affair through WhatsApp and calls. But he rarely initiated the talks. It was his colleague who was after him for talking and going out. Also, there were hardly any outgoing calls from the guy to his colleague; instead, it was otherwise.

"My doubts, however, were confirmed when I closely noticed the chats which had raised questions about the guy's intentions. While chatting, he used 'text language' or shorthand most of the time. Y for why, nt for not, bc for.."

"Behenc.." Akshay murmured but was stopped midway by Diksha's pinch on his arm.

"Because," Rashmi said. "In that particular chat, however, he had used longhand. That portion seemed to be written by someone else. Over a few days, I also saw the guy having frequent verbal spats with his father." Rashmi pointed with his chin at Bhatia. "Bhatia would keep on goading him to leave his girlfriend, as she was always suspicious of his loyalty and didn't trust him. Bhatia further worsened that matter by telling him that his girlfriend had hired a private investigator to gather evidence against him.

"I checked with the girl later to find out who else knew that she had hired me. She told me that it was actually her father's idea to hire a PI. It was clear to me that both fathers disapproved of their children's relationship. Instead of fighting against the couple's choice, they both planned to create this misunderstanding between them. I checked the documents against Bhatia's texting style—he writes in longhand. I checked messages against other family members as well, just to ensure the match. It was a clear-cut case. I got the final confirmation from the guy's colleague, who spilled out the truth after a little intimidating and some casual use of cuss words." Rashmi took a deep breath. "That was some monologue."

"Indeed," Akshay said. "So are we expecting here girl's father as well?"

"Of course. I don't think Bhatia wouldn't have told his partner in crime about their scam getting busted. The girl's father might be on his way."

The iron gate creaked again. Everyone turned their heads toward the CCTV display screen. Priya's father appeared, entering the house. Like Bhatia, Priya's father, too, stormed into the office.

"What do you think of yourself, Ms Purohit?" Priya's father barked. But before he could speak further, his gaze fell upon the tied and injured Bhatia. His expression shifted swiftly from anger to fear. He gulped.

"I have told everything to your children. They might be reaching here soon," Rashmi said.

Akshay finally understood why Rashmi was so busy texting when he'd reached the office.

The couples, too, joined a few moments later. Priya lashed out at both fathers, while the guy chose to remain a silent spectator. Boss, however, was not interested in the drama being played out at her office. She guided them all outside, reminding Priya to transfer the remaining amount today itself.

She reappeared at the door. "Arora," she called him.

Akshay got up and reached her in no time. "Yes, boss."

Her voice was a little louder than a whisper. "I know Diksha is a cute girl and of your age group, but if you're hitting on her, please do not try it in the office hours."

Akshay understood how Priya's boyfriend would've felt of the allegation.

Chapter 6

Rashmi's subordinates left the office at six in the evening. She didn't like to keep them work overtime if there was no need. Akshay appreciated this habit of her. According to him, his previous boss kept his team sitting for hours post the stipulated time just to show his superior that he was working his ass off more than other teams. Corporate culture. She continued to work for the next five hours. Later, she locked the office door and went upstairs to her house, which was on the ground floor, just above the basement.

Her house, like her office, was minimalist. A sofa set, which could accommodate four people and a wooden coffee table with wobbling legs, both belonging to her father's time, occupied the space. The sea green wallpaper that had spanned over the three walls had been faded to almost white, with patches of green. The wall without wallpaper had the doorway and a wide window. A window AC, also from her father's time, stood hanging at a portion of the window.

Rashmi switched the ceiling fan on and sank in the couch. She didn't need to switch the lights on. Darkness gave her comfort and calmness, the desired solitude. It was like a meditation.

She closed her eyes. "My daughter will be a CBI officer," her father's voice rang in her ears. Her eyes popped open. *Not again.*

Her housemaid had already prepared the food a couple of hours ago. As every day, the curry would have gone cold and the bread hard. She trudged to the kitchen. She was in a dire need of caffeine. Coffee was her lifeline. Sometimes when the day was over demanding, she would lose count of the number of coffee mugs she would have. Today, she only had three mugs until now.

She fished out a milk bag from the fridge, poured a cup of milk in the milk pan and put it on the stove. In the meantime, she poured a tablespoon of coffee powder in a cup, half a teaspoon of sugar, added a few drops of milk, and whisked the mixture to make a homogenous, dark brown paste. The milk, by now, was brimming at the edge of the milk pan. She grabbed the pan's handle and discharged the steaming milk into the cup, raising the milk pan up slowly, lengthening the stream of milk, and frothing the coffee inside the cup. The aroma was uplifting.

Perhaps this should help me swallowing the tasteless food.

They said not to consume caffeine some six hours before the sleep. However, she had coffee almost every day before sleeping and she had faced no problem whatsoever.

It was five minutes to midnight and she didn't know when her mind would succumb to sleep. She sat back on the couch, joined her palms together and rested her chin on her fingertips. The street light filtering inside was enough for her to give a faintly illuminated view of the Wall of memories. The wall that fronted the couch was adorned with photo frames, of course from her father's time. "My daughter will be a CBI office."

She closed her eyes.

Rashmi's eyes never left the screen of her HP desktop computer that her father, who was sitting beside her, had bought only a year ago.

On the screen was displayed a PDF file, at the top written — Combined Graduate Level Exam. She scrolled down the list of thousands of roll numbers. The roll numbers were arranged in an increasing order, and she was scrolling down, searching for her roll number.

"My daughter will be a CBI officer," her father would always say, right from the time when she was a child, "like me."

Her father was an officer in the Central Bureau of Investigation—a federal investigative unit under the purview of the government of India— and wished his daughter to follow his suit. As she grew up, she accepted her father's dream as her own. She kept on recalling her father's ambition, and made up her mind that CBI was her ultimate goal. And she appeared for the exam the very year she completed her graduation.

Her hand trembled as he her finger rolled over the scroll wheel. Her heartbeat rose to a crescendo as she was nearing her roll number.

She scrolled down and felt as if she missed her roll number. She scrolled up and looked again. It wasn't there.

Her father sighed heavily. He stood up and put his hand on her shoulder. "It's okay. You never crack it in the very first attempt."

A sharp pang of disappointment pierced her heart. She closed her eyes and allowed tears to trickle down. She wasn't as strong back then.

The notification sound of her mobile phone jarred her back to the present. She squeezed her eyes, screwing up her face, cursing herself of being weak again to surrender to her memories. *Memories are like leeches. If you allow them to stick to you, they will do nothing but suck your blood.*

She grabbed her cell and read the message that she'd just received in the Pi-Agency mobile app.

Her eyes widened as she read it.

Chapter 7

Rashmi's alarm would invariably beep at six in the morning, leaving her sleep cycle limited to five hours or so. Every day when her alarm beeped, she would think to start sleeping early. But a good habit was difficult to adopt and bad difficult to shun.

She got up and poured water in her coffee mug and then threw it in the microwave for ninety seconds and mixed a tablespoon full of coffee powder in the water. She gulped down the black coffee in a single shot.

The curious message she'd received last night would not stop her from going for her morning jog. Prospective clients normally dropped their issues in the message and requested an appointment to meet and discuss the case. If Rashmi felt the case worthy, she would go ahead.

This time, she'd received a message from an employee of Arya Consultants. The employee was none other than the owner's secretary. The secretary straightaway mentioned that Rashmi was hired for a case, but the issue was too personal and critical to replay over an instant message. So, Rashmi had been called in to meet the owner, Brajesh Arya, with one strict condition that she came alone.

After the morning jog, she headed straight to the nearby grocery shop and picked up two pouches of skimmed milk. She set a packet of candies on the counter.

"What is this?" the shopkeeper asked looking at the packet of candies.

"The spare change you are giving me for last twenty days," she said. Shopkeepers in Delhi, or rather, throughout India, had come up with a smart tactic of giving candies for the same price instead of spare change. They knew that buyers wouldn't argue over one or two rupees in change. Rashmi patiently collected the candies until they matched the cost of the milk pouches.

"Are you kidding me?" the shopkeeper dismissed her. "I can't accept these."

"Stop me if you can." She picked up the pouches and left without waiting for shopkeeper's response.

*

Rashmi picked a plain, white casual shirt from her wardrobe to pay the owner of Arya Consultants a visit. She didn't have much option in formal clothing in her wardrobe. She never needed one. She sifted through her clothes but didn't find any trousers. She selected and a pair of indigo washed out jeans and threw those on. She completed her look with her Puma running shoes.

She threw a final look at her petite frame in the mirror. She felt as if she hadn't gained an ounce in past several years. "Your personality doesn't stand out," a guy had once mentioned her in college during a casual discussion. "I'm sorry, but you need to work a lot on your appearance." She was only seventeen, and a negative comment on her physical appearance was hard to deal with. And it did hurt her. But now she felt it was a blessing in disguise. Not having a 'stand out of the crowd' personality was a big advantage in her current profession. With the looks she had she could easily pass unnoticed in a crowd. She could be anyone – a housemaid, a bookseller, a kitchen staffer, a driver.

She tied her straight jet-black hair into a bun. She looked at her conical face and narrow nose with a non-existent bulb. Her shapely lips, she believed, was the only part of her face that she could be happy about. She wore no makeup on her dusky skin— No mascara, no lipstick, no face powder. Dusky, she smirked, thinking of this dubious word. *It's a word devised by the fair-skinned people. They don't want to sound racist, so they created another term for people who don't fall into their shade of skin colour.* "Dusky is the new sexy," a guy had said to her in the final year of her graduation, probably he was hitting on her. It was one of those rare moments when any guy had shown interest in her. For most of the guys (and girls) in her college, she never existed.

Rashmi left for Gurgaon at nine in the morning. Gurgaon, a National Capital Region city in the Indian State of Haryana, adjacent to the Capital, had become a leading hub of both corporate offices and industries alike. South-west of Delhi, at the border of Delhi and Haryana, it was closer to her home which was in South Delhi.

It had been years she visited Gurgaon. When she finally entered, she came across several newly constructed flyovers, labyrinthine underpasses, and towering corporate offices whose glass façades were gleaming under the clear June sky.

The designated meeting place was, interestingly, not at Arya's office. *The matter is personal.* She remembered the secretary's text.

The secretary had asked Rashmi to meet her at some obscure shopping mall on the Golf course road. It took her no more than forty-five minutes to reach the place.

She strolled across the food court. It was devoid of any crowd. Most of the shops had not even opened. *Brajesh Arya doesn't want many people to see him.* She bought a cup of coffee from a shop and took a random table.

A girl wearing a silk formal shirt and a knee-length black pencil skirt approached her. "Good morning, Ms Purohit. I am Pooja Sharma, Mr. Arya's secretary." She extended her hand. "He is going to join us soon."

Rashmi stood up and shook her hand, offering a faint, formal smile.

"By the way, Ms Purohit, I know about you from the time you helped my mother," Pooja said.

Rashmi tried to remember meeting this woman.

"You had helped my mother to find out that my father was a gay and was having an affair with another man."

"Oh yes, I remember. It was Pi Agency's first case. That was long time ago. But I felt sorry for what happened with your mother."

"No problem. My mother has now found another man, hopefully a straight one this time."

Rashmi was amused to see the secretary had maintained the same formal smile throughout the conversation, with absolutely no change in expression. But who was she to judge? She would, too, seldom leak any reaction on her face ever.

She noticed a middle-aged man, in a crisp royal blue suit contrasted with a maroon tie, approaching her. He wore a pair of dark glasses, his head down most of the time.

"Morning." He avoided eye contact and slid the chair across the table out to and took the seat. "I'm Brajesh Arya." He removed his glasses, folded them and placed them on the table. He glanced at his secretary, giving her the cue to leave.

Pooja bade Rashmi 'thank you' and left.

Brajesh Arya rested his arms on the table and clasped his hands. His shoulders were naturally broad, albeit not muscular. His grizzled-hair was swept cleanly to one side. His thick and broad moustache reminded her of her father. He held her with a cold gaze. "Ms Purohit, what I am going to say now is extremely serious and personal."

"It's about the boy. I know," Rashmi said, observing his clasped hands. Clasped hands often meant the person was anxious and was holding himself back, which would make him difficult to say whatever he wanted to. Telling him that she already knew his problem would soothe her mind a little, showing her familiarity. She would often try to deduce clients' problems, like Sherlock, and would be thrilled by their mixed expressions of confusion, shock, and fear.

His fingers loosened. "How… How do you know it is about my son?"

"Your secretary had mentioned last night that the matter was extremely personal to the owner and couldn't be told over messages. I guessed that the matter was scandalous; that's why my client wanted to share it personally. I checked your background, and I didn't find any involvements with controversies, which means it is related to someone close to you. You only have one son—a college student. So clearly, he has gotten himself into serious trouble—a problem which you don't want to become public. That's why you are hiring a PI.

"Now, I categorise problems into two categories—money problems and people problems. Yours is certainly not a money problem. If it were, you would have handled it yourself, so it is a people problem. What sort of people-problem a college kid could get himself into? A relationship. I know some girls would dream of getting into a relationship with a guy born with a silver spoon. And clever girls know how to trap such guys and then blackmail them for their ulterior motives. So it must be a problem of a blackmailing girlfriend," Rashmi finished in her peculiar single-breath monologue. She displayed no emotions on her face, pretending that it was routine job for her to decipher the problems of her client beforehand, but she waited anxiously for Brajesh Arya to confirm her speculations.

Brajesh Arya took a deep breath and said, "Yes, you are right. It is about my son, and he has gotten himself into serious trouble. But that's the only correct part. Everything else you guessed is wrong."

Rashmi gritted her teeth beneath her lips. *Damn. When will my hit rate improve?* She could only wait for Brajesh Arya to tell her about the actual problem.

"He has gotten himself into a trouble which is even more dangerous than a blackmailing girlfriend—blackmail for his addiction."

"Drug addiction. Then you should head to a rehab."

Brajesh Arya let out a deep sigh and told Rashmi that he had been continuously admitting his son to rehab for the past two years, but with no success.

She understood Arya's problem. But she didn't get was how she could offer any help? "So, what are you expecting from me, Mr Arya? Consultation?"

"He's beyond consultation now."

She raised her brows and shoulder together, as if asking 'then what?'

He leaned a little closer toward Rashmi. "I want you to eradicate the problem."

Chapter 8

Though Pi Agency was a newbie in the field of private investigation, Rashmi had encountered a variety of cases in her short career as a PI – cheating spouses, gay father, employees trading confidential information, background checks of brides and grooms—but she had never encountered a client or case like this one. In fact, this case didn't even fall under the purview of a PI.

"Mr. Arya." She paused, thinking how to put across her words to him. "I think you misunderstood what PIs can do and what they cannot."

Brajesh Arya scoffed. "I do understand."

"I doubt it. This... this is the job of police or Narcotics Control Bureau."

"They have a broader motive when it comes to catching the drug cartels," Brajesh Arya said. "They won't hunt for the specific man I want to take down. They will not catch the man who is targeting college kids over and over again into drug addiction."

"How do you know it's the same person who's doing this? And how do you know their motive is to trap the kids over and over again?"

He glared at her with all the fire he had stored inside. "Every time my son walks out of that rehab, he finds himself into the addiction again. Someone is there who's deliberately making the drugs available to the college kids with ease. To break their will power and get back into the addiction."

It's not some unknown man who is responsible for your son's drug addiction, Mr Arya. It's you. Drug addiction was not uncommon among the rich kids of Delhi. These babies born with a silver spoon enjoyed a profligate lifestyle since their birth. Their parents offered them with more than they actually needed. They kept their children away from the hardships of earning money. The lives of these kids were reduced to branded clothes, overpriced cars, and lavish lounges. Soon, their lives seemed worthless and purposeless.

They fell into depression and later embraced addiction. "So, it is a vendetta."

Brajesh Arya leaned back on the chair, hands still clasped. "I declared as much in the first message. The matter is personal."

Rashmi closed her eyes and thought for a moment. "Do you suspect anyone?"

He raised his chin. His face reclaimed the confidence which was lacking until now. "There's a man goes by the name Alphalion."

Had she heard it right? "Alphalion?"

Brajesh nodded.

"Some kind of code name or what?"

"Whether he's one man or a group, no one know. But it is this Alphalion who's supplying the drugs to the kids. He knows kids aren't strongly willed when it comes to addiction, and he takes advantage of that. He's specifically targeting the rich kids, for obvious reasons."

She cleared her throat. "Mr. Arya, you have to understand how PIs work. We dig out information and evidence. We don't catch criminals. We just hand over the evidence to the client, and after that, it is up to the client what he wants to do with it."

Brajesh Arya disengaged his fingers and spread his hands. "That's all I want— find me who the Alphalion is, one who has trapped my son into this hell. Once I have his identity, I'll drag him to the cops."

"Irrespective of the fact he's just one man or a cartel," she added, "there's a risk to life to me and my teammates."

"That's why I am offering you a fee which is beyond what you can imagine. In fact, the amount which I am offering you as an advance is more than what you've ever earned for solving an entire case. And mind you, it's just the ten percent of the total fee."

Rashmi could see the glare in Brajesh's eyes. He was ready to throw any amount at her, which showed how vital this case was for him.

All along her way back to home, her mind kept on replaying her meeting with Brajesh Arya. Even she didn't want to take up the case, the compensation offered by Brajesh Arya made her accept it. Her conscience screamed that she was being greedy and selfish. She was putting the life of herself and her employees in harm's way. But she knew she wouldn't be able to take her agency to the heights she had dreamt of without money. *To hell with 'money can't buy happiness' bullshit.* She knew if she was going to make Pi Agency a premium detective agency, she needed technological assets and more human resource, which could only be acquired when she had money at her disposal. That was the truth which no one could deny. Moreover, this was also the perfect high-profile case she'd been searching for. If she successfully pulled off this case, Pi Agency would attract more clients like Brajesh Arya.

Although she agreed to solve the case, the task ahead was gargantuan. She had to start immediately. She jammed the breaks in front of her house and hoped out. She didn't bother parking her Maruti Suzuki Alto in its designated parking space in the street, and rushed down the stairs.

Chapter 9

Akshay Arora was a software engineer, employed for a few months' stint with an IT firm. The company had a superb reputation, and leaving that job had infuriated his parents. "The job wasn't interesting enough to hold my interest," he'd replied.

"Interesting?" his father had said in disbelief. "What kind of job is interesting? In my thirty-five years of service, I never found my job interesting. If earning money was interesting, the unemployment rate wouldn't have been so appalling."

He couldn't say his father was wrong. A government employee of previous generation couldn't understand what view this generation held of work. The quality of work mattered more. Engineers were leaving jobs of their field and entering into the world of start-ups. The reputation of the firm didn't matter anymore. The remuneration didn't matter anymore. "I can't papa. I don't want to just go that same place every day, unmotivated, doing the same mundane job."

During his engineering degree, he was more interested in reading about things related to coding and programming outside the course books. His grades had never bothered him. This habit continued in his professional life, too. He would do the work in his own style, not according to his team lead's desires. He didn't like the strict working hours. If his job was done, he wouldn't sit a second beyond the stipulated time. He would have frequent arguments with his team lead. When the team lead couldn't handle him, his manager tried to grill him. It turned out to be otherwise. He bore his job for a total of six months and finally slid his resignation across his boss' table.

He would spend his unemployed time on learning mobile app development and hacking techniques. He would go to the openings section of the various start-up websites and search for a software job. A few months later, he would apply for any job he would come across. "You see," his father said, "it's not that easy. It's a cruel world. Eventually, you've to go back to that very mundane job." The truth, however, was that he couldn't go back to his previous employer, too.

One fine day, he came across a job vacancy in a job portal. The name of the organization looked weird – Pi Agency. He would have mistaken it for a mathematics coaching class if he had not seen the full form – Private Investigation Agency – an intelligently contrived backronym of the mathematical constant, Pi. The name of the organisation seemed pedestrian, but the position seemed interesting—a software engineer for a detective agency. *What can software engineer do in a detective agency? Hack emails? Password cracking?* The prospect looked flashy, but beyond his current skills.

The interview, fortunately, was a cake walk for Akshay. The interviewer, a woman in his early thirties, Rashmi Purohit, was also the owner of the company. She didn't ask anything technical. She stated right away she didn't even know the ABCD of programming. All she knew was MS Word, PowerPoint and basic MS Excel. She also told him that he was going to be the second employee of the company. He wasn't sure for how long this woman would be able to pay him. But he had no choice. He didn't want to be a burden on his family anymore. He accepted the offer.

But once he'd joined the agency, he found that his role was not just limited to coding and creating UI. He had to do all sort of PI work, like following the suspects for weeks and months, observing them, and collecting evidence. He was more than a mere software engineer; he was a detective, and had to work like one. Soon, he began to enjoy this job. It was far more enthralling than an IT job, which would have restricted him to a tiny prison cell-like cubicle.

He'd been working for more than a year with PI Rashmi Purohit, but the new case that boss had just presented was like nothing he'd ever come across. His boss had returned from a meeting with a client based in Gurgaon. The new client was a businessman, owned a company named Arya Consultants. He caught a glance at his colleague, Diksha, who, too, looked tensed.

"So, I won't deny that this case is just another case," Rashmi said in her usual impassive tone. "It's risky, perhaps detrimental. But it is what it is. Brajesh Arya is just the kind of client we were searching for."

Akshay and his colleague nodded.

"We better get our asses to work without wasting a second." She stood and took a position in front of the white board. She picked the black magnet marker stuck at one corner along with blue, green, and red ones. She wrote 'Alphalion' at the top and 'Rohan' at the bottom of the board, leaving a gap between the two same as the height of the white board. "This" – she tapped with the butt of the marker on Alphalion – "is the central problem of the case." She dragged the marker down to Rohan. "And this is where our investigation will start."

"So, we'll start with Rohan," Akshay said. "Interview him." Starting with Rohan was the logical step. Rohan was where the problem started.

"That was what supposed to be the first step," Rashmi said. "Unfortunately, Mr Arya denied. He doesn't want his son to know that his addiction has bothered his father to the extent that he had to hire a private investigator. I then asked them about the people who were involved with his son in this drug ring. He gave me three names." She turned and wrote the three names on the white board an inch above Rohan: Varun Mehta, Adi Luthra, and Karan Shukla. "Rohan's friends, his classmates. I'll start interviewing them one by one."

Akshay had thought that boss would assign some work to him and Diksha as well. He looked back at Rashmi with eager eyes.

"I've a job for you as well." Rashmi laid her eyes on both of them. "Spend your time around Rohan's college, in the areas where students hang out. *Tapris* and *dhabas*. Talk to them. Try to find from where they get *stuff*. You both are smart enough. I don't need to explain anything. Am I clear?"

They nodded in unison.

Chapter 10

After their quick team meeting, Rashmi asked Akshay and Diksha to search for news articles, blogs, and whatever they could get on the internet related to the drugs problem in Delhi. They got to work immediately, and by the end of the day, they came up with a thick stack of A4 sheets.

Normally, Rashmi would sit in the office for hours after both employees left, but today, she left the office. She put the pile of printed articles on her couch and took her favourite brooding spot.

The couch in her living room was placed along the wall, and across the room was the Wall of Memories. Every night, when she got home, she would commit herself to not stare at the wall of photographs, the reason she didn't switch the lights of living room on.

Her sight fell on several photo frames hanging on the wall. In some, she was alone, but in most, she was with her father. The wall of photographs or Wall of Memories – as her father would call it – had been her father's idea. He'd started it when Rashmi was born and maintained placing the photographs as she grew up. It became a timeline of his family's life.

There were a few empty spaces amidst the frames. They were darker in colour than the rest of the wallpaper. There had been photographs there before—the photographs that had her mother in it, but Rashmi had removed those photos from the wall. She didn't want to remember the reason, and that was why she always tried to keep herself away from the wall of photographs. "You're doomed, girl." She often thought about removing all the photographs. She knew it was not right, but she couldn't stop herself from seeing them over and over. It was like an additction. *Memories are like leeches.*

She shrugged off the memories and picked the prints that her employees had left for her. "Read even if you don't like to read," her father would say. "You will learn things that will prove useful when you least expect them to be." Not again, Papa.

She had never mastered the habit of reading. She wouldn't mind reading a news article or a blog. In fact, she liked to keep up with current affairs. But reading a five-hundred pages book was exhaustive, daunting.

The first article reported the areas that were the drug trafficking hubs of Delhi. It included the upscale areas like Saket, Greater Kailash, crowded places like Airport, Old and New Delhi railway stations, and shady ghettos like Seemapuri and Majnu ka Tila.

She let out a big yawn by the time she finished the first article and then looked at the pile of papers. "Sorry, Papa. It's too boring."

Chapter 11

Rashmi caught hold of Varun Mehta in a cafeteria near the college. She asked him to spare some time. When she shared why she was here, Varun paled.

"That was just one time," Varun said, holding the paper coffee cup tightly. Rashmi feared that Varun might squeeze the cup and spill the coffee over himself. "And I just accompanied my friends. I didn't do drugs."

"You don't have to worry," Rashmi said. "I am not going to tell anything to anyone."

He looked around. "We did it a few times, but it was all for fun."

Rashmi took out a small notebook and started scribbling. On a new page, she wrote the date, time, and the interviewee's name.

Varun bent forward, boring his eyes on the notepad's page.

"I forget things quickly," Rashmi said. "That's why I have to make notes about everything." The truth, however, was that she had a habit of recording all her conversations and observations, with date and time. "I have just one question for you. Where did you buy the drugs from?"

"It wasn't me," he responded instantly. "Karan used to get it. I think he knew some drug peddlers. He used to bring them in a yellow envelope."

Blame shifting, Rashmi thought. People would often shift the blame to someone else to escape the trouble. "Okay. So you were with Rohan right from the start?

"I was there only for a few times. We were a group of four friends: Rohan, Adi, Karan, and me. That was two years ago. Karan's company was a bad influence, so I stopped hanging out with them. But Rohan and Karan had developed a good friendship. Those 'drug parties' turned into drug abuse. Rohan's father came to know about his addiction and sent him to rehab. When he returned, he started hanging out with Karan again, and the same thing repeated. Now I think he has understood he has ruined his life. He has stopped hanging out with Karan, but I think it's too late now."

Rashmi noted down the details in bullet points. She wasn't just writing down what she was listening to—she also wrote what she was observing in Varun's statement. "Okay, Varun," she said. "One last question. Do you know anything about Alphalion?"

Varun scrunched his brows. "Alphalion?"

"Apparently the guy who supplied drugs to you."

"Ma'am, I have nothing to do with Rohan. I don't know any drug peddlers or dealers. You better contact Karan."

Rashmi shut the notebook closed. "Thank you for your time, Varun."

*

Rashmi followed Adi Luthra after college. He didn't live in the college hostel but in a PG near the college. He was alone. He headed for a tapri nearby.

A Tapri was essentially a makeshift tea stall, which would sell more than just tea. Students would have tea and snacks and would combine them with cigarette.

Adi ordered a cup of tea, kept it beside him on the wooden bench, and lit a cig when Rashmi approached him. When she told him why was she here, he too was taken aback like Varun Mehta.

"It's been more than a year I've met Rohan," Adi said.

Rashmi sat on the bench, the tea cup between her and Adi Luthra. She only had the morning espresso today. She craved for coffee. "Doesn't matter. I want to know from whom you used to buy the drugs."

He scratched the back of his neck. "I don't remember. It was Karan, I think, who used to bring the stuff for us. Or may be Varun. I don't remember. That was some two or three years ago."

She turned, facing him. Adi Luthra still didn't look at her. "Rohan might not be a good friend of yours. I don't want you to think of him as a friend, but as a fellow student, as a human being."

"He has a rich father, ma'am. He can still do well in life without a degree. He can afford rehabs and medications. I, on the other hand, don't have such luxuries."

Rashmi knew the kids wouldn't tell her anything even if they knew. They were at the end of their graduation. They were also aware about Rohan's predicament. A small mistake and they would lose their degree. "Do you know Alphalion?"

His head spun sharply toward her, and he looked at her for the first time. "What's that?"

"The supplier of drugs."

Adi shrugged. "Could be. These peddlers have fancy names. I think Karan told us once a name."

Rashmi bolted upright.

"But it was something else," Adi said. "Certainly not Alphalion.

She didn't get much information from Varun Mehta and Adi Luthra. But one name was common between both – Karan Shukla.

*

Karan Shukla was a hard man to find. He didn't attend college for next two days. His classmates weren't aware of his whereabouts. She then enquired his hostel mates when she found he was in Bhopal to meet a girl he'd found on Tinder. When he was back the third day, Rashmi caught him right outside his hostel.

"I heard you were looking for me," Karan said. "I was in Bhopal, attending an interview."

Rashmi noticed the ease with which he lied.

"I'm glad you've taken up this job, ma'am," Karan said. "Those bastards need to be sent to jail soon."

"That's right," she said, "and I'm sure you gonna extend your full support."

"Of course."

"So tell me from whom did you buy the drugs?"

"Who told you that I used to bring the drugs?" Karan asked.

"Let's say I just found it," Rashmi. "I'm a private investigator. It's my job."

"Varun?" he guessed, shaking his head, snickering. "Fattu."

"Sorry?"

"Nothing," Karan said, suppressing his indecorous smile. Unlike Varun Mehta and Adi Luthra, he seemed to be comfortable and confident.

"I asked you something," Rashmi induced sharpness in her tone. "From whom or where did you get the drugs?"

"Ma'am, you believe the words of Varun Mehta and Adi Luthra." He scoffed. "Varun Mehta lost fifty-thousand in trading. He was broken and feared to ask his father for money. I bailed him out. And this Adi Luthra. He hasn't met his widower father for once in the past three years despite his father living nearby in Laxmi Nagar. He disappears for days. Some say he does some odd freelancing work for god knows whom. So if you're judging me by the testimonies of these guys," – he shrugged – "I can't help."

Rashmi crossed her hands. "I'm not writing a biography on Varun Mehta and Adi Luthra. I trust no one but my own common sense. So I repeat my question again: where did you buy the drugs from?"

He looked around. "Can we take a walk?"

Karan didn't want to stay closer to the hostel and other students while talking about drugs. "Alright," she agreed.

"You can get them from a lot of places. *Jhuggi jhopri* clusters are the hot spots. Then there are the peddlers of Seemapuri— they are the kings of smack."

Rashmi knew the places where one could find drugs. Surprisingly, the drug trafficking areas in the national capital were available in abundance. From the slum resettlement colonies to New and Old Delhi railway stations to her own urban locality of South Delhi, one could find peddlers anywhere. What she wanted from Karan was where exactly he bought the drugs from. She fixed him with a fiery glare. "I think you're not getting my question."

"I.. I.. you want to know from where did I buy them?"

She didn't even give a nod this time, only bore him with her gaze.

"I bought *maal* a few times from a peddler. His name's KD. He used to supply drugs for our college students. And most importantly, he was available on call. Used to be convenient for us."

"I want this KD's contact number."

"See, ma'am, I don't do these things frequently. I just bought from him a few times."

Rashmi took a deep breath and counted to ten. "I've heard this shit a lot in past two days. Can I have his number?"

Karan gulped. "Sure."

Chapter 12

Rashmi met her employees after three days. She didn't take updates from them in these days. She would never spoon fed them. She wanted them to be independent. She would definitely help them if they would ask her for help, but she wouldn't teach them how to approach any job given to them. She gave them a free hand. "I give a rat's ass how you get the results. Just get them."

It had been three hours since her morning espresso. It was now time for white coffee. She brewed a cup quickly, sprinkled some sugar in it and swallowed it in a matter of ten seconds. Akshay and Diksha would still request her to install a coffee machine in the office, but she would always refuse, calling it a waste of money. It was indeed. And it wasn't just a one-time investment. She had to pay for every month for maintenance and coffee beans, too.

She put the ceramic coffee mug into the sink, wiped her mouth, with her knuckles and rushed down to the basement.

Akshay and Diksha were sitting on their respective chairs, their heads bowed and eyes glued to their smartphone screens.

"Morning, guys," she said.

As they heard her voice, they got to their feet in a split second. She motioned them to sit back, walked around the table and took her seat. "How was your investigation?" She let them share their findings first.

Akshay shifted in his seat, preparing himself to answer her question. He was a smart fellow. Two or three inches shorter than six feet, he had an athletic build. He would always be eager to leave office before six, reasoning that he would find an empty gym if he would reach before six. He wasn't beefy like those oil-coated bodybuilders, but had a toned up figure. When he walked, his hands remained spread as if he'd stuck a block in his armpits. A thing, or rather disorder, Rashmi believed, common with all bodybuilders. The most annoying thing in his overall look was his hairstyle – long and voluminous at the top and suddenly trimmed down to millimetre length at the sides and back. And not to forget the thick beard extending annoyingly below his chin, making his face oblong.

Akshay tugged his ears and said, "Students were not that forthcoming whenever we spoke of drugs."

She nodded softly.

"'I don't know' or 'he knows better' or 'it was just one time' that was the kind of answers we got." He glanced at Diksha. "She'd almost given up, but then I found a girl."

Diksha winced. "No, I hadn't given up. I was just… I was just tired."

"Whatever," Akshay said. "So this girl said there's a professor who is rumoured to sell drugs to college students."

A bitterness filled Rashmi's mouth. "Professor?"

"Yes," Akshay said. "It sounds disgusting. She wasn't comfortable sharing with me his name. I offer her to exchange numbers. Chatted with her for two days –"

"He was hitting on her, actually," Diksha interrupted. "This information he got is just a coincidence."

Akshay rolled his eyes. "His name is Vishwas Puri. Department of Economics. Rohan's department."

Rashmi propped elbows on the table and intertwined her fingers. "So we've got a contender for Alphalion."

Akshay gave a vague shrug, whereas Diksha remained neutral.

Rashmi outlined her end of the investigation, her observation on the three 'partner in crimes' of Rohan. She then walked up to the white board and wrote KD (S1) and Professor Vishwas Puri (S2) above Rohan's friends' names, where S1 and S2 stood for Suspect 1 and Suspect 2 respectively.

"So what's next, boss?" Akshay asked.

"We've got KD's number." She put the cap lid back to its place and punched it with her palm. The lid sat on its place with a click. "Let's call him and see what he has got."

Chapter 13

No, this is not real, Akshay thought, seeing his clean shaven face in the mirror. *This is all a bad dream.*

After boss's instruction, he'd called KD, asking for maal. KD had disconnected for the first time. It took Akshay some time and effort to convince him that he was a college student, just looking for something beyond whisky. KD then seemed to be convinced and asked him to meet today evening at Majnu ka Tila.

"Trim off that chest-length beard before you go to meet KD," Rashmi had instructed him.

"It has taken me three months, boss," Akshay retorted.

"You have to look like a college student. With this nest hanging beneath your chin, you aren't going to look like one. KD won't take you for a student."

Please don't do this to me, boss. He pictured his face melting.

He managed to steal a glance at Diksha. He could see nothing but a devilish grin on her face.

Thankfully, boss allowed him to keep his quiff as it was.

His phone chimed. It was a WhatsApp message from Diksha: "Send me your selfie."

"Do you want me to use foul words?" he replied.

She sent an array of laughing emoticons. "As if I've asked for nudes." More emojis followed.

Akshay switched the data off.

For my job. He took a deep breath. *For my detective career.*

Majnu ka Tila was a colony in North Delhi named after a fourteenth century Iranian Sufi, nicknamed "Majnu", or "crazy lover." He had met first Sikh Guru – Guru Nanak, the founder of Sikhism – here on a tila, or mound, and hence, the place got its name Majnu ka Tila.

It was an hour ride from metro. The place was bustling with traffic in the evening. Akshay could also notice a police station. It was exactly the opposite of the kind of places where peddlers normally made deals, and that made him wonder why KD had chosen such a place.

Akshay waited for KD in front of Gurudwara Majnu ka Tila Sahib. This place brought back some sweet and bitter memories from the past. He would often come here with his former girlfriend, Smriti Bansal. Smriti was a cute girl, pretty much like Diksha. She was actually very much like Diksha. About same height, same oval face, hair straight at the top, streamed down until shoulder, or a little below, albeit not purple at the ends like Diksha had. She was a little leaner than Diksha, probably because that was a couple of years ago. If he would check her present picture, perhaps she would be of same build as Diksha.

It was only a six months affair. She wanted the commitment a little too soon. How could he have committed to a long term relationship, a relationship that she expected to transform into a marriage? That was where the problem started. She thought he was using her. He was, honestly, not. The relationship ended on a bitter note.

He still remembered her. But she was now taken. He'd stalked her on FB a few weeks after the breakup and she was already into a new relationship. He stopped himself to stalk her after that. He didn't have the courage. He was not ready to absorb the truth. When Diksha had said that he was hitting on the girl from Rohan's college, she was partly right. He yearned for a relationship, especially after his former girlfriend got a new guy now. Someone with whom he could share everything, go out on dates, have late night talks.

A sharp honk pulled him out of his thoughts.

A scrawny figure on a bike stopped in front of him. His face was hidden beneath a helmet and a tinted visor, making his head look disproportionately larger than the rest of the body.

"Akshay?" the lanky guy asked.

"KD?" Akshay responded.

No one said yes and no one nodded, yet they both understood they met the right guy.

"You want *cut?*" KD's voice was muffled beneath the helmet.

Akshay recognised the street slang for adulterated heroin. He ran his gaze toward the police station. If he was caught here, he would land in some serious trouble. He nodded, nevertheless.

KD cocked his head toward the pillion. "Come with me."

Akshay hesitated. He wasn't sure where this guy would take him. There were places in the city which were not safe for a common guy like him, the kind of places which where playground for people like KD. Or worse.

He climbed on the pillion, and looked back. He was not on his own.

*

Rashmi was ready to fire the engine of her Honda Activa (it was actually Akshay's) as soon as she noticed a motorcyclist passing by Akshay a couple of times. She was annoyed to see Akshay being lost in his thoughts, not paying attention to his surroundings. He should have spotted the motorcyclist. Like Rashmi, who from almost three hundred meters away was sure the motorcyclist was KD.

Rashmi wore a ¾ helmet with a clear visor. It was getting dark and a tinted helmet would leave her practically blind.

She sparked the scooter to life as she observed KD tilting his head back.

KD kicked his motorcycle start and turned right. Rashmi twisted the throttle and begin the trail.

KD manoeuvred the motorcycle in the crowded streets, his thumb seemed to be pushing the horn switch in a quick pulses.

Rashmi didn't remember when she last rode a two-wheeler. Her father wouldn't allow her to ride one. He thought it wasn't safe for females to ride a two-wheeler in Delhi. She wasn't as skilled in snaking the vehicle between the pedestrians and hawkers. Yet she made sure she wouldn't lose the sight of the motorcycle. KD steered the motorcycle sharply to the left to an alley. As Rashmi neared the corner, she realised the alley was vacant. There wasn't anyone but KD and Akshay.

She stopped before the turn and almost reflexively, hoped down and pulled her bag out from the luggage space. It was her surveillance bag.

She dug out a monocular from the bag. She preferred monocular over binoculars during surveillance. A monocular was a smaller, compact version of a telescope. It would fit in her palm. She wouldn't have to use both hands as in the case of binoculars, and therefore, more efficient.

When she would do the surveillance by her car, she would assign particular places for her investigating gear. The camera and a camera stand would always be kept on the front seat. Smaller items like binoculars, a power-bank, and recorders would be kept on the back seat. A notepad and pen would always be kept inside her breast pocket. By doing this, she wouldn't have to search for items when she had to leave the car hastily. In situations like today, she had prepared a surveillance bag.

She jumped out of the scooter , propped it on a side stand, and ran up to the edge of the alley. She gazed down the street and saw the motorcyclist had stopped.

She placed the monocular in front of her right eye. She turned the knurled ring on the body of the monocular, adjusting the focus on KD and Akshay.

KD removed his helmet.

Chapter 14

The bike's seat was as miserable as its owner's clothes. Dirty and speckled with holes. The way KD was suddenly jamming his foot on brake pedal and twisting the throttle, Akshay realised how his girlfriend would have felt when he would do the same. The only difference was that she wasn't sitting behind a drug peddler.

He wondered whether Rashmi was following them. He ducked and glanced into the motorcycle's rear-view mirror.

Nothing.

He'd trust in his boss. She wouldn't leave him alone with a drug peddler.

KD stopped the bike in a desolated alley, and they both got off.

"What does this mean?" Akshay said.

"We couldn't do business in such a crowded place," KD said. "There was a police station."

"You brought *maal?*"

KD removed his helmet. He then slid his hand inside his pocket and pinched out a stapled packet of the size that could easily hide in his fist. "Two grams. I am sure you know the rate."

Akshay had done his research. He handed KD two five hundred rupees rolled notes. He imagined how his father would react if he found his son was buying adulterated heroin.

"I've sold like this after a very long time." KD smelled the bills. "Business is running quite cold these days." He stuffed the notes inside his jeans pocket.

"Sold like this?"

"Yes, sold like this. Out in the open, in the streets, for hard cash."

Akshay just gave a nod. He wanted to know more, but at the same time didn't want to make it apparent to KD. "Coppers are quite vigilant these days."

"Cops aren't a problem," KD dismissed.

"So you aren't getting the supplies."

KD's dark brown complexion further deepened. "What's your problem? You've got your stuff. Now fuck off."

Yeah, I should. If he would irk KD more, his ass would be in some serious trouble. "I don't have anything to do with your business, brother. My friend Karan had suggested me your name. He says he is your regular customer."

"I don't know any such fucker?"

Doubts clouded Akshay's mind. Did Karan really buy from KD? Or it could also be possible that Karan hadn't shared his true identity with KD. "Karan Shukla from Sri Krishna College of Commerce."

"I don't remember everyone's name." KD turned toward his bike. "I still have some stock left with me. Won't last longer."

Akshay considered this was the moment to play the gamble. "Then I think I need to contact Alphalion."

KD stopped, and whirled, his helmet clenched tightly in his hand. He trotted toward him, his strides longer and faster.

Akshay felt things were going to go bad from here. He closed his fist, pulled his shoulder blade back, and tightened his core, like he did before every working set during his workout. If it was going to be fist fight, Akshay was fairly confident he would overcome. But there was a high chance KD was carrying a pocket knife.

KD stopped inches before him, his tip of the head reached only until Akshay's nose. "How do you know Alphalion?"

"Everyone knows him," Akshay made up on the go. "They call him the kingpin of drugs."

KD clenched his jaws. "You're a student. Stay away from people like this. Even street peddlers like me dread him." He covered his head with the helmet as if Alphalion was watching him from somewhere.

Akshay was tempted to ask more, but stopped himself. "Never go overboard when you are questioning a potential suspect," Rashmi would often say.

Chapter 15

As soon as KD left the alley, Rashmi appeared at the corner, making herself visible to Akshay. Akshay was unmoved. "Arora," she called out, her hands motioning him to run to her. "Run, idiot," she muttered.

On her command, Akshay darted toward her. As he reached, he swung his right leg and took the pillion.

Smart guy, Rashmi thought. Seeing the revving engine of the scooter, Akshay would've figured out what she was going to do next.

Close tail.

She left a gap of two car lengths from KD, which was a standard whenever she would tail her surveillance subjects. She wouldn't often shadow them by a two-wheeler. It was always either by car or foot.

"Boss," Akshay said, his mouth inches away from her ear. He still had to yell in order for his voice to reach her amidst the blaring horns and roaring cars. "I think he's not Alphalion, but he knows who is."

"Why do you think we're following him?" she had to yell, too. "Do you think he works for Alphalion?"

"I'm not sure. But he looked afraid when I spoke of Alphalion."

Then KD could be a member of some rival gang. And Alphalion's gang could be more powerful than KD's. Or KD wasn't a gang member at all.

KD stopped once for relieving himself. When he resumed, he jumped every traffic signal he came across, forcing Rashmi to break the law, too. It was a peak hour and losing the sight of KD for even a thirty seconds signal would let him slip in the ocean of vehicles.

From Majnu ka Tila, KD was moving further east. Rashmi guessed he was heading toward the localities of north-east Delhi. She was certain when she saw the overhead metro track and

Red Line metro stations such as Shahadra, Mansarovar Park and Jhilmil. She didn't remember if she had ever been to this area of Delhi. She pictured the map of Delhi. They were riding on GT Karnal road and if they continued straight, they would cross Delhi-UP border and would reach Ghaziabad – a city in the state of Uttar Pradesh, adjoining Delhi.

KD, however, took a sharp left toward the colonies. She wasn't sure which area was this. Her doubt later cleared when she spotted a Police station mentioning – Seemapuri.

Seemapuri was a sprawling slum, a trash dump, and a workplace for rag pickers where they would sort recyclable and reusable waste. One of the prints found by Akshay and Diksha reported eighty per cent of the kids working here were addicts, some were as young as seven. Peer pressure, drug use by family members were some of the underlying causes. Rag picking was also a factor. One of the addicted kids in an interview said he had taken drugs because his friends told him it would help him fight against the strong stench of the waste.

Dusk had faded away, turning the sky deep blue. The dingy bylanes of Seemapuri had minimum lighting, the street lights glowing in patches. The streets were wide enough only for a single car to pass. The buildings on both sides were three or four storeys, mesh of electrical cables hanging low across them. A strong stench of trash and sewer and shit filled her nostrils.

KD zigzagged the bike in the streets quite skilfully. It was his territory.

"Keep an eye on your surroundings," she instructed Akshay. "We might be running into a trap."

Akshay's silence gave away his fear, and Rashmi might have further elevated his fear by saying they could land in trouble.

KD stopped in front of a building abruptly. It was a three-story building. He parked his bike at the front, removed his helmet, and walked inside.

Rashmi stopped some fifty meters before the house.

"What do we do?" Akshay whispered.

Rashmi asked him to get off the scooter. "Follow him."

"Are you sure?"

She marched ahead. Akshay followed her.

From the entrance, Rashmi noticed that the residential building from inside had a central, open air courtyard and tenements all around. She guessed there were eight tenements on each floor. She caught a glance of KD walking on the second floor. She watched him enter a tenement.

"Let's go," she mouthed.

They bound up the stairs to the second floor. Soft-footed, they reached the passageway cum balcony, which connected all the tenements on the second floor. A clothesline ran all along the length passageway on which the residents had hung their washed clothes to dry.

She was only about a couple of feet behind the tenement in which KD had entered. There was a wooden door at the entrance and window alongside. The windows were shut, but KD didn't close the door completely when he'd entered.

Rashmi held a hand up, gesturing Akshay to halt, while she stepped ahead gingerly. She took a spot near the door, she motioned Akshay to remain where he was, closer to the staircase, in case they had to flee. His eyes flashed fear, and keeping him away from the door would make him feel better.

She stuck her back one the wall, right at the edge of the threshold and listened to the conversation going inside. Whom KD had gone to meet? Was she going to find Alphalion inside today?

Chapter 16

"Are you out of your mind?" Akshay's father couldn't believe Akshay had joined a private investigation agency. "You're a goddamn software engineer."

"And I'm going to work like one, Papa," Akshay had said. "UI and some backend job."

"But why a detective agency? Do they even exist in real life?"

Even Akshay had no idea private investigation agencies existed in India in abundance before he appeared for an interview for Pi Agency. "What's the difference? I'll do what I was doing in my previous employment. I'm no sleuth."

Except that he was absolutely wrong that day. Now standing inside a slum settlement, he felt he was better off with his first job.

Boss was sometimes brash, like today. They shouldn't have really come to this place, let alone trespassing the resident of a drug dealer. If anyone would find them here, trouble was the least thing they could fall into.

Someone on the ground floor suddenly started playing Punjabi rap songs, and his heart almost jumped out of his mouth. Boss, on the other hand, was calm and composed, all her attention fixed inside the room.

Akshay, too, focussed his attention inside the tenement.

"You told me you'll leave these things," a female voice said, seemed to be like an elder woman. May be fifties.

"I've already left, Maa" KD said.

Maa? She is KD's mother. It's KD's home.

"Then what is this?" the woman sharpened her tone.

Rashmi inched toward the door. She seemed to sneak inside the room, trying to find what KD's mother was showing him.

No, no, Akshay cried inside his head.

The tenant on the ground floor played Punjabi rapper, Badshah's song, *Yeh Ladki Pagal hai Pagal hai.* This girl is crazy.

KD was silent for a few seconds, then said, "I got a call from a guy from Delhi University. I thought to sell the leftover stock."

"You promised me you'll leave these things," she cracked.

Metal clinked inside the room followed by a sound of water pouring inside a steel glass.

"Then how am I going to earn the bread for us," KD snapped. "Do you have any other way out?"

There were a few moments of stand-offish silence between the two.

"I am going to return all the leftover stock you have," KD's mother broke the silence. "He's called me to know what you're doing with the computer he gave you. I told him we aren't going to do these things anymore. I'll return everything he's given to you back."

KD clucked his tongue. "Why are you messing with him, Maa? You know what he'll do to us if we don't comply."

"And do you know what will the police do to us if we are caught? I'm not going to help you anymore."

The next thing Akshay heard was steel glass clattering on the floor and splash of water hitting the ground.

"If you've decided our fate," KD said, "then there's no need to discuss anything with me."

"He has called me to meet tomorrow below Mahipalpur flyover at midnight. You'll accompany me."

KD said nothing.

Footsteps came toward the door.

Fear formed a knot in Akshay's throat. He shot a glance at his boss. Rashmi's pupil shifted toward the drying bedsheets, hanging like curtains on the clothesline near the railing.

Instinctively, they lunged together. They slipped behind the bedsheets, sticking themselves to the railing, accommodating themselves in whatever narrow space was left between the hanging sheets and the metal railings. The bedsheets were still damp and smelled of washing powder.

The music stopped, leaving the building in a muted silence. *Wow. What a timing.* He held his breath.

The wooden door squealed and the footsteps sounded clear. Akshay was sure his thick back profile was visible on the bedsheet. *I shouldn't have done those heavy barbell rows.*

Footsteps faded and then rang in the staircase. KD appeared in the open area on the ground floor and then went inside in another tenement, probably in his friend's place. They slipped back to the passageway.

KD's mother emerged at the same time from the threshold as Rashmi and Akshay. The buxom woman wore a *salwar kamiz,* and a *duppatta* covering his head and neck. Her eyes rested on them, and she frowned, appraising them top to bottom. The residents wouldn't expect strangers in their building often, particularly people like Rashmi and Akshay who belonged to the portion of the capital which was in stark contrast to their ghetto.

Rashmi fished out her phone in a split second and stuck it to her ear. "We're here," she paused, pretending as if she was listening to the other end of the call. "Oh, no." She put her hand on the back of her head. "I think we are at some wrong place." She gestured Akshay to move. "Not a problem, we're coming."

The woman's eyes with arched brow followed them as they scuttled out of the building.

Chapter 17

When Rashmi entered her basement office, she found only Diskha. "Where's Arora?"

Diksha shrugged. "Normally he's punctual."

Rashmi took her seat.

"You guys worked late yesterday?" Diksha asked.

"Not much actually. He should've got back home by nine, I guess." She stared at the white board, paying attention to the gap between KD and Alphalion. Perhaps this gap wasn't this big now. She also considered S2. She wasn't sure if professor held any importance now. She turned back to Diksha. "Was he out until late with friends last night?"

"I don't know if he's any friends here. He never mentioned about them ever."

"And what about you?" Rashmi asked. She realised she rarely asked her employees about their personal life, partly because she didn't like sharing her personal life with anyone.

"I've a few friends here, from my previous employment. I go out on weekends. Mainly for shopping. And golgappa."

Rashmi couldn't stop a smile appearing on her face. She remembered if she had ever gone out with friends in all these years. Never. She had broken contacts with all her friends after college. After… after…. *You're doomed, girl.* She forced herself not to think about it. Not in front of Diksha.

Akshay appeared at the doorsteps. His head hung low.

Rashmi realised he was hiding his new look, a forced change, actually.

Diksha's eyes widened. She stifled a giggle.

Akshay glowered at her. "Boss, if she's going to make fun of my new look, I'm resigning."

"I didn't even utter a word," Diksha said.

"I can sense you're laughing inside your mind."

Diksha made a face. "So you're a mind reader now. Boss, we do need such detectives."

Akshay shook his head and sat on his chair. He ran his hand around his cheeks and chin. He was probably missing his beard. Rashmi noticed that he'd also trimmed his hair short and turned it into spikes. He was looking younger.

Rashmi got up and picked the markers. "We found out yesterday that KD gets the drugs from someone. And he sells it to earn money. Apparently, KD's mother too knows about her son's wrongdoings. They were talking about someone who appears to be their drug supplier.but they never took his name. KD and his mother are going to meet that man, which, I believe" – She circled Alphalion thrice with red marker – "is him."

"What about the professor that we'd found about?"

"I found about," Akshay snapped.

"I approached that girl first."

Rashmi shushed them. "Is this an office or a kindergarten?"

Akshay and Diksha sat straight, their mouths sealed, their eyes fixed on the white board, as if they'd just been chided by the teacher.

"I had given a thought about our professor. Whether he was really involved in selling drugs to the students. I think it's a campus myth. Every college has that. Myths about teachers, students, hostels. False information that you get from the grapevine. It was quite prevalent in our times when there were no smartphones. Imagine how it would be now when WhatsApp messages propagate like a nuclear chain reaction."

"So we strike off professor's name from the suspect list?" Akshay asked.

Rashmi smirked. "A detective should never strike off any suspect. Though, the most important part of our investigation is witnessing KD and his mother's meeting with their supplier in Mahipalpur, but this afternoon, I'm going to do some fielding on Professor Vishwas Puri. Does anyone have anything to add?"

Diksha raised her hand. "Arora looks like a child now in this new look." She cracked up even before she finished.

Akshay glanced at her with cocked head, his face flushed red.

Rashmi let a smile appear on her otherwise deadpan face. "No, he looks like a human now."

Chapter 18

Professor Vishwas Puri's resident was in Defence Colony, which was a twenty minutes ride from Rashmi's place. Professor would return only in the evening, but Rashmi decided to garner some information from the people in the vicinity.

She talked to security guard, launderer and housemaids about Vishwas Puri. He was a recluse. His wife had left him a year ago. Everyone quoted a different reason. The security guard said the professor wasn't faithful. The housemaid said the wife wasn't faithful. The girl from Rohan's college told Akshay that both husband and wife weren't faithful. *It's amusing how people think of adultery is the only reason for broken marriages.* They'd a son who lived abroad and had not come to meet them in years.

Rashmi killed time for another ninety minutes before Vishwas Puri arrived.

He pulled his white sedan into the parking space in front of his house. The four intertwined rings at the centre of the wheel gave away the brand of his car. An Audi seemed to be quite a luxury for a government college professor. But that couldn't prove anything of its own. The door opened and two legs grounded on the gravelled ground. Then he held the car's body and pulled himself out with great effort. He was in his mid to late fifties. He sauntered over to the other side to the passenger seat and took out his black leather laptop bag that seemed to be another branded product. He wore a sky blue, cotton, full-sleeve shirt – which had gone untucked from sides – and a charcoal grey formal trouser. His leather shoes were pointed and shining like graphite. His medium length, straight hair had turned grey and his fuzzy beard was completely white.

Rashmi had found out beforehand that his house was at the second floor. He lived there as a tenant for eight long years and all of a sudden, one fine day he bought it from the owner. It would've cost him a great sum of money to buy a property in one of the plushest localities of Delhi, and she doubted if he had enough money in his savings to buy a property like this.

Rashmi waited for another twenty minutes before she climbed the stairs and pushed the doorbell switch. It rang with a commonest of all doorbell rings – ding dong. There was a brass lion door knocker on the polished wooden door, which she doubted if anyone ever used.

Vishwas Puri opened the door and stopped it half away seeing a stranger.

"Professor Puri," she said, "I am Rashmi Purohit. I'm a Private Investigator."

Vishwas Puri cocked his head, confusion sweeping across his square face. "How may I help you?"

"I want to have a word with you, with regards to a student of yours."

Vishwas Puri pulled the door, making way for Rashmi to enter inside.

The professor hadn't switched the lights of living room on. He let the living room naturally lit up the grey evening light filtering in through the glass window. He directed her toward a chocolate brown couch, offering her a seat. "Private Investigator?" his voice was buoyant. "Like detective or something?"

The professor had changed to cream Kurta Payjama and a pair of black PU sandals. The sking below his sallow eyes, Rashmi observed, began to hang.

"Right," Rashmi said and waited for him to sit.

Vishwas grabbed the armrest and rested his bottom and back on the couch delicately. He seemed to be having back issues. "I never knew private detectives existed in real life. Anyway, how may I help you?"

"Sir, I'm here to speak about a student of – "

"Sorry." Vishwas got up, pushed a switch from the switch board, and plopped into to the couch.

A chandelier above her head with rose gold metal rods and more than ten filament bulbs lit up, bathing the living room pale yellow. She glanced left and right. The walls were adorned with quality wallpaper and expensive showpieces and paintings. A dark wood coffee table with a storage space underneath was placed in front of her. A few envelopes were scattered in the storage space, most of them seemed to be credit card and bank statements.

"Sorry, you were telling me about a student," Vishwas said.

"I'm investigating the case of a student of yours who is struggling from drug addiction. The addiction became so bad that he'd to be admitted to a rehab. But every time he walks out of the rehab, someone is there to pull him back again into substance abuse. My job is to find who the perpetrator is."

She searched for a reaction on Vishwas's face, but not even a single muscle flickered.

"Then perhaps you should get hold of his friends," Vishwas said.

"I'm getting hold of all the people who could be involved with my client."

"Involved?" He gawked at the word. "Are you implying that I'm involved?"

"I haven't said that. It's what you're implying."

"What does a professor have to do with a drug-addicted student? Rather we often raid their hostels for alcohol and cigarettes and sometime girls."

She decided to probe in more. "I've heard things about you."

Vishwas Puri huffed from his nostrils. "I bet you heard most of it from the students." He seemed to be playing along.

She nodded vaguely.

"And I bet you believed all of it." He showed his teeth for the first time.

"Why not? They are the ones who live with you from dawn to dusk."

He exhaled. "Look Ms – "

"Rashmi Purohit."

"Ms Purohit. I belong to an era when even speaking of beer was considered a taboo. A sin, in fact. I've no idea about any of this. Even if I'd heard about it, I would've ignored it. We all teachers ignore such things. You know, with all this freedom of this a that bullshitting around, we don't want to be seen in a bad light by prohibiting students from anything."

She shrugged. "Fair enough. One last thing. I've a name. Alphalion. Does it ring any bell?"

She waited for a reaction. Surprise. Fear. Anything. But professor's face leaked nothing. He stared back at her like he was staring a blank wall, and shook his head.

"Alright." She got up. "Thanks for your time. I may need to bother you again."

He grabbed the armrest again and pushed himself to his feet, grunting. "May I know who this kid is?"

"Sorry. I'm bound by a privacy policy."

Rahsmi scooted down the stairs. She had kept her cars four houses away from Vishwas Puri's house.

As she was driving back home she analysed the investigation she did until now. KD had direct link with Rohan, through Karan. So he was an important contender of being the Alphalion initially. But as things turned out, he didn't have much stock to regularly feed to Rohan. But he did know Alphalion. Dreaded him, in fact. As for professor Vishwas Puri, she wasn't too hopeful of getting anything significant from this meeting. She was expecting a similar response from him as she'd obtained from Rohan's friends. Professor's lavish house, however, says something else. He'd suddenly become rich and then his wife left him. It could mean he earned the money in some wrong way. But that didn't mean it was from selling drugs. Even if she assumed that professor had sold drugs to his students, it could've been a one-time affair as it was only one girl's testimony, and that too wasn't authentic.

At this stage, KD's meeting with his supplier seemed to be the most promising part of her investigation.

And she had to be ready to make most of it.

Chapter 19

Pooja Sharma had enough of the LIIT topped with three tequila shots today at their quarterly get together. One of her colleagues could drop her at her house, but Brajesh Arya thought it wasn't prudent to leave his secretary in this state with anyone else. He was already getting late, for Rohan was at home waiting for him. He'd hired a nanny for his son's company, but Rohan wouldn't stay long without her. His employees were of a good character, but he didn't want to take risk. A misstep and his company's image would be at stake.

Pooja stopped the car four times along the roadside to throw out all the excess alcohol she had had. "Sorry, sir," she panted. "Normally it doesn't get this ugly." She wiped her mouth with a kerchief. "I think there was some problem with the quality of the food or alcohol."

He nodded. Right. *Everyone blames the quality of the alcohol whenever they puke and not their over indulgence.*

When he finally dropped her home, he jammed his foot on the gas, piercing the traffic, violating all speed limits.

He had a two storey bungalow in Green Park, having a parking space for two cars and a lawn of the size of a cricket pitch, which was small but enough for two people in the house.

He entered soft-footed inside the house. The living room's lights were off. There were two more rooms in the ground floor of which one he'd converted into a home gym. He didn't remember when he last used the treadmill. It was only used in rainy season to hang washed clothes.

He climbed up the stairs and found Rohan's room lights were on. *Surprising.* Rohan should've slept by now.

When he opened the door, he found Rohan sitting on the bed, his knees folded to his chest and his hands wrapped around his knees. The nanny was sitting beside him, hugging him. "It's okay," she was whispering into his ears.

When the nanny saw Brajesh, she got up. "Bhaiya, Rohan

saw something in the mobile phone and is shivering since then with fear. I've asked him several times, but he isn't telling me anything."

Brajesh rushed to him. "What happened, beta." He ran his hand on Rohan's head.

Rohan eyed the nanny.

"Give us a moment," Brajesh said.

The nanny left them.

Rohan showed him his mobile.

He'd received a WhatsApp message from an unknown number. It was a video. When he played it, he realised it was the video. His hand trembled. He hit the pause button and looked at Rohan.

"Alphalion," Rohan murmured.

Brajesh Arya's phone rang. He fished it out from his coat's pocket and checked the display: Unknown number. He swiped the call button and put it on his right ear.

"Mr. Arya," the now familiar robotic voice said, the voice of Alphalion. "I thought you were a smart man. I warned you against going to police, so you went one step ahead and hired a private eye."

A chill gripped Brajesh's spine. *How does he know I've hired a PI.* "I... I... it's a mistake. I haven't – "

"Oh, shut up, Mr Arya. I know everything. I think you aren't content with the payment amount."

"I'm arranging the money. You know I can't arrange all the money at once. I'll go bankrupt."

"Yet you have all the money in the world to hire a private detective." His robotic voice didn't have any emotion, yet it sounded threatening to Brajesh.

"The investment amount is double now."

"Please, I cannot... please listen to me..."

The line got disconnected.

He wiped the film of sweat formed on his forehead.

Rashmi Purohit, he thought, *you are my only hope.*

Chapter 20

Chander Kala, a forty-three-year-old woman, ran a small grocery store in Seemapuri. Four years ago, she had come to know about her son's illicit business—illegal drug peddling. At first, she was furious at her son, but KD had later convinced her that he was doing it for their own good. The money they earned from the grocery shop barely covered their bread and butter. They needed something more and bigger to earn their livelihood.

Not only had KD got a nod from his mother to continue, he had also convinced her to get into the business. She would take the stock from different sources and distribute it to other street peddlers like her son. Their distributors were often busted by the police, seizing huge amounts of drugs, due to which they'd faced heavy losses. Hence, a woman like Chander working as a distributor would be the least suspicious.

Chander began to make a reasonable amount of money from the distribution. Her son, too, was making money by filling the streets with drugs. KD had even got the rag-picker kids into addiction. Everything went fine for three years. But problem started when the drug dealers had stopped dealing with them. She knew, like all wrong things, this would come to an end soon. Before she got into trouble with police, she wanted to end it forever.

Mahipalpur was cramped up with motels and hotels. A village situated in the vicinity of National Highway and Indira Gandhi International Airport, the villagers cashed in on the locational advantage by adopting the hotel business. Now, Mahipalpur was a village of hoteliers.

It was quarter past twelve, but it didn't look like it was late at night. The area was vibrant and glittering with the colourful lights of the hotels. Being close to the airport, the area was flooded with passengers and taxies.

Chander had already reached Mahipalpur at half past eleven and waited under the Mahipalpur flyover. She was holding a small jute bag in her hand, its mouth zipped up, inside which was the leftover stock of drugs. She had a primitive Nokia phone in the other hand, at which she was quickly looking, expecting to receive a call. She waited for half an hour more, but there was no sign of anyone.

Passing by people and taxi drivers stared at her in a bad way. A man even came closer and asked, *"Kitney mein de rahi sey"*. She felt disgusted at herself. It was all a consequence of her past misdeeds. *Karma, they say, always comes back.*

When it was close to one, she deemed it was not safe to stay there any longer. As she was about to leave, she saw someone charging toward her. She believed it was him, and she stepped forward. But the figure seemed different, looked like a woman, but its walk seemed like a man. Something is not right. She whirled 360 degrees, but spooked out finding a young boy right behind her.

*

Rashmi and Akshay had reached Mahipalpur at eleven. They parked their car in front of a hotel, from which the view of Mahipalpur flyover was clear, and they waited inside the car. They saw KD's mother climbing out of an auto-rickshaw and taking a spot beneath the Mahipalpur flyover. Her face was covered with her *dupatta* today. but the *salwar kamiz* was same as the other day. She carried a jute bag. KD was nowhere to be seen. Rashmi hoped he would join later.

The clock kept on ticking, but neither KD came, nor the man with whom KD's mother was supposed to meet today. She waited and waited, and when it was about one, she noticed KD's mother appeared to be leaving.

"Arora, " Rashmi said, unlatching the door, "make sure she doesn't get away."

Rashmi hoped out of the car and approached KD's mother. The woman's sight rested on her, and she looked unsure.

As expected, seeing Rashmi approaching her, the woman turned the other side to escape, but found Akshay barring her. KD's mother stumbled back, seeing Akshay. She turned back to

Rashmi. Her eyes and forehead were the only visible parts of her face. Deep frowns creased her forehead.

"Who were you waiting for?" Rashmi stood inches away from her, quickly getting to the point and intimidating her.

"Who… who are you?"

Rashmi gritted her teeth. "I know what you are carrying in your bag. I know what you and your son are up to. Just answer my question. Who were you waiting for, and who do you work for?"

The woman swiped her dupatta down, her lower lip trembling. "I have stopped doing these things. I just came back to return whatever I've left with."

"Just tell me who you were going to meet!" Rashmi hissed.

"I don't know his name. He contacted my son a few months ago, gave him a computer. He told us that the whole drug game has changed, and my son doesn't need to go out in the streets and to sell drugs anymore."

"What does that man asked your son to do with the computer?"

"I don't know. Even my son doesn't understand it well. He was happy being a street peddler. But these are dangerous men. If he doesn't agree to their wishes, they will kill us."

"Is this some gang?"

The woman nodded, albeit unsure. "He came with some big guys."

"Do you recognise this name Alphalion?"

"No," KD's mother rasped.

Rashmi pursed her lips and stepped forward. KD's mother stumbled back, hitting the flyover walls. "You say those men are dangerous. Then you don't have any idea what can I do to you."

"I don't know," the woman broke into sobs. "I'm not lying."

"Where's your son?"

The woman slowly began to sob.

Rashmi winced. She needed to meet KD if she wanted to learn more. Her options were limited. She had to meet KD and find out who gave him the computer and why? Too many dices had been rolled suddenly, and the number of outcomes had been spiked up. She grabbed the woman's wrist. "Let's go."

The woman stood her ground. "Where?"

"Home sweet home."

Chapter 21

The woman's name was Chander Kala. Chander told Rashmi that she was an immigrant from India's eastern neighbour, Bangladesh. Chander didn't mention, however, if she was an illegal immigrant, neither did Rashmi ask. Chander entered India some seven years ago, stayed in West Bengal for a while, then Bihar, and then travelled all the way to Delhi, where she worked as a rag picker. With place, her name changed. She didn't tell Rashmi her real name. Her husband, she told, was a drunkard, would often beat her and take her hard earned money. She left him. At the age of seven, her son joined her in rag picking work. It wasn't a choice. It was a compulsion. Like her son's drug peddling work, which too, she reasoned, was out of compulsion. KD didn't like living in slums. He wanted to live in a better place. And he started doing drugs business. They earned a good some of money in coming years, and got to rent a tenement.

Along with Chander and Akshay, Rashmi reached Seemapuri. In her last outing, Rashmi had learnt that the compressed by-lanes of the slums would not permit Rashmi's car to enter. They parked the car outside and took a walk to Chander's house.

The reek of sewage welcomed them as they tread their way through the dark streets to Chander's lodging.

The building was black as ink at this hour. The waning moon, thin and sharp as a steel sickle, wasn't bright enough to brighten up the world naturally. Rashmi lit the flashlight as they climbed up the stairs.

Given the kind of guy KD was, she expected dealing with KD wasn't going to be a cakewalk. "Arora," she said, "I believe you can handle KD if things turn ugly."

Akshay took some time to nod.

"You aren't looking confident. C'mon, you once told me you bench hundred pounds."

"Boss, there's a difference between hitting weights and hitting people."

Rashmi spilled the flash on the wooden door. A stainless steel lock of the size of a tennis ball shimmered.

Chander looked around. "He's not come back." She retrieved a bunch of keys tucked at her waist. The keys jingled in the dead of the night as she inserted a key into the lock.

Chander stepped in and switched the tube light on. Rashmi and Akshay followed.

"No, no, no," she murmured, looking around, as if something was amiss. She went up to a rusty algae green almirah kept at the corner and opened it. "He has taken all his clothes."

Rashmi kept her hands on her waist and exhaled. She thought she was going to get some information on Alphalion today. But now KD was gone. She turned back toward Chander. "You told me about a computer."

Chander went back to the almirah. "It's still here".

It was a dark grey HP laptop, lying at the top shelf. There was no charger. Rashmi went ahead and retrieved the laptop. She didn't need Chander's permission.

Chander looked at Rashmi helplessly, but she was in no position to stop her. She looked more worried for her son.

Rashmi heard a commotion in the ground floor. Footsteps resounded in the staircase. She guessed there were at least four persons coming up.

She handed over the laptop and jute bag to Akshay. "Disappear."

Chapter 22

Five men, all in khakis, stormed inside Chander's house. Rashmi recognised the lead man as soon as he came under the illumination of the tube light.

Inspector Mohit Sherawat.

He had been at the same college as Rashmi. Both had the same ambition of getting into the CBI. They were competitors. Neither of them had passed the CBI exam, but Mohit still made it into Delhi Police. He started as a sub-inspector and moved up the ladder quickly to become an inspector.

Mohit reminded her of her failure, her father's unfulfilled dreams.

Shock swept across Mohit's face as he registered Rashmi's presence. He clapped and guffawed. "My goodness, RP. Of all people in the world, I expected to see you here the least."

Rashmi's mind raced. *Why's Mohit here? Someone must have tipped police about Chander and KD.* "I'm investigating a case."

Mohit had bulked up in all these years. Massive chest, meaty arms, and cannonball like shoulders like rugby players, if Akshay was here, he would've have taken some pointers from him. With his towering six and a half feet height, he looked like an Egyptian soldier.

Mohit snickered. "Investigating?"

His smile was annoying. She said nothing. She knew Mohit loved to humiliate her.

"Now if you may please excuse me," Mohit said, "I've a more pressing matter at hand."

"You're interfering in my investigation, Mohit."

"You're interfering with *police* investigation, RP. I know how trivial your cases are, so seal your mouth and go back to your rat-hole of an office."

Anger seethed through her hearing the spiteful remark about her office. But she swallowed the rage. Mohit's uniform stood between Mohit and her.

"I've got a tip. Her son is a drug dealer."

"He's not here," Chander said, panting with fear.

Mohit gestured to his subordinates, and the constables rushed inside.

Rashmi's pulse jumped. *I'm sorry, Arora.*

Chapter 23

When a male voice mentioned of police investigation, Akshay realised police was here. Someone tipped police of KD and it didn't look a coincidence. One of the men was Mohit, and apparently, he was known to boss.

Chander's house had one room and a kitchen. There was no bathroom. Perhaps there was a common bathroom on each floor. *If police are here, then they will surely search through the whole place.* He scanned the kitchen. No place to hide. His heartbeat rocketed. His eyes fell on an overhead storage space. It was about three or four feet in height.

He climbed the kitchen platform. The storage space was at the shoulder height. He pushed the laptop and the jute bag inside. He grabbed the edges and pulled himself up, swinging his legs and placing it on the floor of the storage space. He then crawled inside. The cemented surface was coarse and it scraped his skin. His elbows seethed with pain.

There was an iron trunk inside, a few utensils and clothes and blankets.

He heard footsteps and voices approaching toward the kitchen. He crawled and curled up behind the iron trunk. He then pulled the laptop and the drug bag.

The policemen threw the utensils on the floor, the cacophony of metal hitting the concrete filled the space.

"He's not here," one of the men said.

Akshay wondered why the policemen were throwing the utensils on the floor. Were they expecting to find KD inside a pressure cooker?

"Wait," other man said. "There's a storage space here.

"Let me have a look."

Akshay heard a grunt.

"Push me up."

His heart pounded. He curled himself tightly. The trunk was

not big enough to hide him. *Shit.* He grabbed the blanket and clothes and heaped them above his body.

It was all dark now. He didn't have claustrophobia, but he was still afraid. He struggled to breath beneath the thick layers of clothes. He could hear his heart hammering beneath his chest.

"You see anything?" one of the policemen said.

"Hold on," this voice was just outside the mouth of the storage space.

Akshay held himself tight. A flicker of the movement and he was gone. He couldn't imagine what charges would be placed against him if he was caught with a bag full of drugs and a laptop… he still had no idea what was inside it. More than getting caught, he was worried about what would he answer to his father.

Hiding beneath blankets in June drenched him with sweat. His t-shirt hugged him from all around. He loved sweat only inside the gym. A bead of sweat rolled down from his hairline to his eyebrow, stinging his eyes, but he couldn't wipe it right now. He squeezed his eyes.

"Nothing is here," the policemen sneaking inside the storage space said.

Akshay heard a grunt and foot striking the ground. The footsteps then receded back to the front room.

"Listen, woman," the man whom boss had called Mohit said, "tell me where your boy is and I'll be soft with both you and your boy."

"I'm not lying. I really don't know," Chander pleaded.

"Then I fear," Mohit said, "I've to call in women police and take you in custodial interrogation."

"She's not lying, Mohit," boss said. "I'm also after her son. Probably he's fled after knowing someone has tipped off the police."

"My dear, RP, I believe you too need a custodial interrogation."

Boss didn't say a word.

Akshay heard everyone walking out, the door being bolted. He threw the blanket around him and filled his lungs with air. His troubles weren't over yet. If everyone was gone, it meant he was locked inside.

As he was about to jump out of the storage space, he heard the wooden door being open. He crawled back inside.

Footsteps came in the kitchen. "Arora."

Akshay was never so happy hearing his boss's voice. He felt like hugging her when he would get down.

"Boss," he said, crawling out at the edge, "I'm here."

When he appeared at the mouth of the storage space, he saw a smile appearing at Rashmi's face. It was the first time he saw her smiling.

"Arora," she said, "you are truly a gem of a guy."

*

It was three and both Rashmi and Akshay had their eyes fixed on the laptop screen. Rashmi's sleep had vanished. Arora, however, looked weathered. But she couldn't wait till morning to scan the laptop. There must be something that could help her find Alphalion.

Akshay opened the search bar and started hunting through files and contents for 'drugs'. With no results from that, he entered 'cocaine', 'LSD', 'marijuana'—no luck.

Rashmi grabbed the laptop and dragged in it front of her. She punched in street names like '*maal*', 'cut', 'charas', 'ganja', 'joint', '*malana* cream', '*chitta*', and whatever words she could recall that related to drugs— a .txt file popped up.

She opened the file and saw these names listed in the file, their weightage and rate listed alongside. *What's this? Some sort of inventory file? But why would KD need to do all this?*

"Can we find the creator of this file?" she asked.

No response came from Akshay. She noticed Akshay had dozed off. "Arora," she shook her.

Akshay's eyes popped open. "Sorry, boss."

She moved her eyes to the right bottom corner of the laptop screen. Three ten. She rested her head against the back of the chair and closed her eyes. "Arora, we have had enough for the day. I think we should call it a night."

"Yes." Akshay rubbed his eyelids. "In fact, we should call it a morning."

Chapter 24

Rashmi woke up from a dead sleep when the alarm beeped. She slapped her hands over the bedside table to find her mobile phone and stop the alarm. It was six in the morning—her usual waking time. She could only afford three hours of sleep. Her mind was more drawn toward finding clues from KD's laptop, and it wasn't letting her have a sound sleep. She kept on lying in bed with her eyes closed, trying to sleep again, but soon realised that she wouldn't be able to sleep anymore.

She got up and looked at herself in the dressing table mirror kept beside the bed. Her sleep-deprived, swollen eyes made her look even uglier—as if a dusky complexion, a body thin as a stick, and an angular face like pointy-toed shoes weren't enough.

She prepared her espresso and gulped it down like a medicine. She hadn't bothered to change her clothes in the night, and had gone straight to bed. After waking up, she still didn't bother to change them.

The mornings of summer were windless and hot. She strolled down to the basement. The closed office felt like vacuum, and made her sweat. She thought for a moment to switch the AC on, but she reminded herself of last electricity bill that had burnt a hole in her saving account.

She opened the laptop's lid. Last night was quite eventful. Even after so much hustle and struggle, she began to doubt whether KD's laptop would yield anything important.

She kept her finger on the power button. She curled her finger and pulled her hand back. She shut the laptop lid and closed her eyes. She opened her eyes again and pulled the pile of articles that Akshay and Diksha had printed for her, and which she hadn't read, save for the first one.

Drug trafficking, she read, was the third-largest business in the world. In India, drug abuse had grown only in the past decade. Drugs were initially thought of as something which only the upper income classes could afford, but with economic growth, the middle class, too, entered their shadowy world. Students saw it as an experiment, actors enjoyed the indulgence, and working professionals used them to cope up with stress. Yet however one encountered them, dipping one's toes in would soon lead to drowning in a sea of addiction.

In recent years, drug seizures by the Narcotics Control Bureau and police had also increased, but it couldn't be taken as an encouraging development. The quantity of drugs captured in every bust had also increased, which meant the flow of drugs into the country had also gone up, which in turn indicated an increase in the number of users as well. Moreover, the seizure only accounted for roughly ten per cent of the total drug imported to the country.

The drug problem, Rashmi thought, was not a rare phenomenon in India. Several actors and singers had fallen into drug addiction. Politicians had been accused of encouraging drug trafficking in their states, using it as an incentive to attract voters. People assumed drug abuse is largely limited to the northern state of Punjab, thanks to the elaborated media coverage and a certain Bollywood flick, but the fact was that this vulture gripped the entire country in its claws.

In the midst of reading, Rashmi turned her face away. Her eyes were burning from lack of sleep. Caffeine could delay sleep, but couldn't provide the rest the human body begged for. She rested her head back on the chair and ran her fingers through her hair.

She began to doubt herself. She wasn't sure whether taking up this case had been a good decision.

Chapter 25

Diksha was running late today. She hated to be late. She didn't want to give Arora that rare opportunity when he reached earlier than her. She didn't have enough time to dry and style her hair. She tied it into a ponytail. The tail dyed purple at the ends looked funny. Chuck it. She threw on a peach spaghetti top and a pair of dark blue ankle jeans. She completed her looks with black platforms heels.

She'd rented a PG close to the office, close to seven minutes walking distance. When she was out, she noticed men ogling at her. *What,* she thought, *you've a problem with this spaghetti top, too?* Last Saturday she wore slinky little black dress at a friend's birthday party, and all her friend's male friends were stealing glances at her, some even looked as if they would eat her alive. Her parents and friends had warned her that Delhi was not so easy for a girl to survive. And she'd experience it every day.

She was born and brought up in Ahmedabad, a city in the Indian state of Gujarat. Her father had started hunting for a groom right after her graduation. To delay the marriage, she did MBA. But her father resumed the hunt the day she finished her post-grad. "Twenty-three isn't an age to get hooked up, dad," she had said.

"It takes time to find a good guy, beta," her father said. "If I begin now, maybe I find a guy in next two years."

"And what if you like the very first guy you meet?"

"Then I consider myself lucky."

She knew if she would stay in her hometown, her father would tie her to a guy in a matter of six months. She found a job in an ad agency based out of Delhi. Her father didn't like the idea, but her mother supported her and she succeeded to leave Ahmedabad and shifted to Delhi.

Her luck ran out in six months. The ad agency handed over pink slips to many employees, mostly the senior management and those who were less than a year old. She was jobless in an unknown city. She didn't share it with her parents, for she knew her father would call her back. She hunted for a job while surviving on the money she'd earned in past six months.

It was then fate took her to Rashmi Purohit. She mistook Pi Agency to a PR agency and had applied for the job of a marketing expert.

Within a week of her new job, Diksha figured out that Rashmi Purohit was a cocky woman. She was passionate about sleuthing, but she had no idea about running a business. Akshay Arora, the IT expert, was her right hand. Diksha's job was, however, only limited to running ads on social media, posting articles on LinkedIn, SEO, sending festive wishes to existing clients. She had once advised Rashmi Purohit to send sweet boxes to clients, but her boss was a tight-arse.

She checked the time. Two minutes past nine. *Fuck. I'm two minutes late.* She hurried down the stairs.

Akshay hadn't come yet and she breathed a sigh of relief. Rashmi Purohit, surprisingly, was present today even before her. Her hair was untied and frizzled. Her white cotton shirt folded up until her elbows looked crumpled. Her heavy-lidded eyes were glued to the laptop screen.

Diksha knew her boss and Arora had gone to witness the meeting between KD and the drug dealer. She was curious to know how events had turned out. She focussed on the laptop and realised that no one in the office had an HP laptop.

Chapter 26

Rashmi studied the .txt file again and again. The list of drugs gave away nothing. She then closed the file, right clicked on it and selected 'properties' option. The Author field mentioned 'Admin' and in the Company, PEGDEL. Google search gave different anagrams of the word PEGDEL. She the tweaked the search to 'PEGDEL company in Delhi', but found nothing.

Her eyes burnt of lack of sleep. She covered it with her hand for a moment.

"Morning, boss," she heard Diksha's voice. "Started early today?" Diksha kept her laptop bag on the table and rolled her chair to her. "Arora didn't come today?" she asked, looking around.

"You missed a lot yesterday, girl," Rashmi said.

Diksha put her bag on the table and opened her laptop. "I was forced to miss it."

Rashmi sensed the complaint in Diksha's tone. And Diksha was right, partially. She didn't get detective work as often as Akshay did. Most of the time, she handled the social media marketing for Pi Agency. Rashmi would never involve Diksha in any situation where there was a slightest hint of danger. And whenever activities had to be carried out at night, Diksha was strictly prohibited. Diksha had tried several times to involve herself, as she had yesterday, but Rashmi would always refuse. Not that Diksha wasn't capable of those missions, but Rashmi had to be practical, and she knew Diksha was more vulnerable to harm.

"You weren't made to, my dear. It's just that Akshay and you have different roles to play."

"And I never get to be the Robin."

"Robin?" Rashmi chuckled.

"Yes. Batman and Robin."

Rashmi gave a hearty laugh.

"Fine." Diksha crossed her arms and looked away. "If you

aren't going to consider it a serious issue, then there's no point in discussing it further."

Rashmi stifled her laugh. "You don't need to be my sidekick. Your job is more vital to the business. It's because of your marketing work that we get the cases at the first place. If not for you, Arora and I would be sitting idle in this office."

Diksha seemed to calm down at that. Rashmi knew how to handle Diksha's childishness; she had been doing it for past six months. Normally, she wouldn't have allowed Diksha to talk back like that, but she also knew how to assess the mood of her subordinates and keep a balance between strictness and leniency.

Diksha's reaction got her reminded of her own conversation with her father when she had decided to join a private detective firm.

"Private investigator!" her father said in disbelief, "You want to become a private investigator?"

"Yes, you heard me," Rashmi said.

After not getting through the Civil Services Examinations for the fourth time, Rashmi had given up on joining CBI. Later, she'd come across a newspaper ad about a vacancy in detective agency of Delhi.

Her long-lost ambitions resurfaced. If not a public investigating officer, she could very well be a private investigator.

"It's not that simple, beta," her father said. He would never to speak to her in stern voice, let alone reprimand her.

"Why? Because I am a girl?"

"Partly."

"Do you know Rajani Pandit and Taralika Lahiri?" she asked.

Her father shook his head.

"They are the top woman private investigator of India, and you know they are of your age group? They started as a PI in the 80s. So why can't I in the twenty-first century?"

"It's not safe for a woman to be a PI," her father reasoned.

"And would it have been safe had I been a CBI?" Rashmi shot back.

Father's eyes found the floor.

Rashmi realised she shouldn't have said that. She hadn't been able to fulfil her father's dreams. Her father never showed his disappointment outwardly—and somehow, that was even more disheartening. She was disappointed with herself, and she knew her father was, too.

He looked back at her with a smile on his face. "If you are happy, I am happy."

The memory bought a smile on Rashmi's face.

"Okay," Rashmi said, seeing Diksha waiting for her response. "Let me tell you what happened last night."

Chapter 27

Rashmi narrated the entire story of last night's adventure, and Diksha appeared glued to the narration as if a thriller movie was being playing out in front of her eyes. "Really," Diksha said, "Arora did that? He doesn't look that brave."

"And now we are stuck at this .txt file," Rashmi said. "I'm sure we can find more in the drive, but I'm too tired to manually go through each and every file."

"Lemme do it for you." Diksha rolled on her chair and reached beside Rashmi. She grabbed the mouse without even asking her and opened the drive.

There were only two folders, named 'Pic' and 'Video'.

Diksha opened the 'Pic' folder. A quick glance to the image thumbnails and Rashmi noticed most contained exotic models with little or no clothing. Diksha rolled down and there were photographs of KD and his friends at different tourist places of Delhi. In many photographs, Rashmi observed, KD wore a blue wrist band having a logo that looked like a cheap imitation of Twitter logo.

"I think I've seen this logo somewhere," Diksha said, rubbing her chin.

"Is it some wrist band brand?"

Diksha shook her head.

Diksha then switched over to the vids folder. As she opened the first video file, the office filled with a loud moaning of girl.

Rashmi didn't need to see what the video was and she closed it right away. "Gee."

Diksha giggled. "I don't find it unusual. A guy's laptop without porn is abnormal."

First twenty videos were disgusting pornographic material. Rashmi displeasingly went through each file, while Diksha kept on giggling. She then came across a video file which seemed to be a randomly recorded video from a mobile phone. The video panned from bottom to top and stopped mid-way. The flooring and walls looked like that of KD's house. The camera could only capture until a man's chest. He wore a black polo and in his right wrist, he sported the same blue wristband.

"Believe me, this is going to change your life," the man said.

"Hmmm…" The voice on the other end sounded like KD's. He was probably holding his mobile phone casually, with the video recording on, so that the man wouldn't suspect him. The video ended abruptly.

"What was that?" Diksha mused.

"I think this is the guy who gave KD the laptop," Rashmi said. "Probably KD was too scared to continue, so he ended the recording abruptly."

"So this man is Alphalion?"

Rashmi was asking herself the same question. "We don't know yet. KD's mother didn't know his name. And she didn't know anything about Alphalion."

"This man wore the same wristband as KD."

"Apparently, laptop wasn't the only thing he gave it to KD."

Diksha scrunched her nose. "I still feel I've seen this logo somewhere?"

"Some clothing brand?"

"I've seen it very recently?" Diksha raised her chin and squeezed her eyes. "Wait." She opened her eyes and grabbed her phone. "It was Wednesday," she murmured, scrolling down the screen. "No Thursday." She tapped on the screen. "That's it." She showed Rashmi the screen. It was a text message that said an order was shipped by a courier partner named Pigeon Delivery.

"Pigeon Delivery?" Rashmi asked.

"Yes." Diksha snapped her finger. "I bought running shoes online last week, you know I've gained two kilos and got to start running in the morning. Anyway, the delivery guy had a big bag on his back. The back had this logo."

"Pigeon Delivery," Rashmi said PEGDEL. A renewed wave of energy surged inside her. "That's my girl."

Rashmi did a quick Google search. The logo was indeed the same. "Why would a logistics company make a wrist band?"

"Some companies make their own publicity-targeted swag and accessories for customers and employees," Diksha answered. "My previous company had them, too." She appraised the paused footage of the man in black polo. "Do you think this man in question works for Pigeon Delivery?"

"I think the man in question owns it," Rashmi said, staring hard at the Twitter-like logo. "You wanted some detective work, right?"

"Of course," Diksha chimed.

"Dig out whatever details you can about this company and its owner," Rashmi said, and got up. "I haven't bathed since morning." She pinched her collars. "Haven't even changed clothes since last night."

Chapter 28

After Rashmi cleansed herself of the sweat earned last night from the misadventure at Mahipalpur and at KD's home and the stench of Seemapuri's slum, she took her favourite brooding spot. She needed some time alone, to think about where the case was heading. She had some clues, and now she needed to connect them into a seamless thread. She made a mental flow-chart of events and their outcome. Rohan – Karan – KD – laptop – Pigeon Delivery.

How Pigeon Delivery was involved in the drug trade?

"I've sold like this after a very long time," she remembered KD's words. *"Out in the open, in the streets, for hard cash."*

Something sparked inside her mind. *Drug trade has become a risky affair, given the numbers of busts the authorities have made lately. So why not get it sold by someone who wouldn't be suspected at all?*

Delivery boys.

After the outburst of e-commerce in India, one could see plenty of delivery boys running around through the city all the time. They would easily go unnoticed by authorities. What an ingenious idea? Pigeon Delivery had probably set up this new drugs model, and fusing peddlers like KD into this model.

But it was just a conjecture at this stage. Nothing more than a wild guess. She needed more information.

She sprang up from her chair and bound down the stairs.

Akshay had already arrived, joining Diksha in searching for Pigeon Delivery details.

As Diksha noticed Rashmi's arrival, she got up with her laptop and charged toward her. "Boss, I have a few details on Pigeon Delivery." Her excitement was at its pinnacle.

"Hold on, hold on," Rashmi said, and took her seat. "Yes."

"Pigeon Delivery is a fairly new organisation," Diksha said, "and operates only in Delhi NCR. It has just one warehouse, situated in Udyog Vihar, Gurgaon, and a corporate office at Rajendra Place. It was founded by Ankit Malik. He is an MBA from IIM Rohtak. Started with an international bank, hauled his ass there for three years before embarking his own business." She took a deep breath. "And I found it all alone without any help from Arora." She stuck her tongue out to Akshay, who still looked exhausted.

"If Pigeon Delivery and Ankit Malik is our suspect, we can check out their warehouse. They could probably store drugs there," Akshay said.

"It's not that easy to walk into their warehouse, or any warehouse, for that matter," Rashmi said. "I have another way out. First off, I must make sure that the man in the video is Ankit Malik. And then I've to find a way to infiltrate into Pigeon Delivery.

Chapter 29

Rashmi had to visit the slums of Seemapuri third time in a matter of a week. This time Rashmi felt the smell of trash had softened a bit. Or she had gone accustomed to the stench.

Chander was released by Mohit the next day in the absence of any evidence against her. KD was still lost. When Chander saw Rashmi at her place again, she broke up, "Why are you after us? What wrong did we do to you?"

"I'm just doing my work," Rashmi said. "I mean no harm to you or your son."

The tears streamed out freely from her eyes. "Please bring my son back. He didn't do anything wrong. He just sold a few grams for our livelihood."

Rashmi scoffed. "He didn't do anything wrong? He's just spoilt a kid's future."

Chander wiped her tears. "Please bring my son back."

"I'm trying to get the perpetrator caught." She showed her phone to Chander. The screen had photograph of Ankit Malik fetched from social media. "Is this the man who gave your son the laptop?"

Horror gripped Chander's damp face. Her nod was more like a shiver.

Rashmi pulled her hand back, squeezing her phone in her tight grip. She was both angry and content.

Because she had just found who Alphalion was.

Chapter 30

"Good God, Detective Rashmi Purohit," Purushottam Purohit, Rashmi's uncle, said, "I thought I would never get to see you in this lifetime ever again."

From Seemapuri, Rashmi travelled all the way to Noida to meet her father's younger brother, Purushottam Purohit. Rashmi understood the sarcasm in her uncle's comment. She hadn't seen her uncle since her father's demise. She hadn't met any of her relatives in those five years. She then realised she couldn't remember any close relatives other than her uncle.

Purushottam was a customs officer with the Indian Government. He was five years younger than his elder brother, Dheeraj Purohit, Rashmi's father. He was shorter and bulkier than his brother. His face, however, closely resembled that of her father, save for her father's broad moustache. If her father had been alive, he would have looked similar to how her uncle now looked.

"Anyway," Purushottam said, "have a seat. How's Pi Agency doing?"

"So-so," Rashmi said. "I have a new case, which, in the truest sense, is the kind of job I had expected to do when I started the agency."

"Great. I am happy for you."

"And I need a little help," Rashmi came straight to the point.

"Oh, how did I guess?" Purushottam said. "What else could be the reason you came to me after these many years?

She exhaled. "Uncle, I don't want to give you any excuses about why I never visited…"

"I am not asking for any excuses," Purushottam spoke over her.

Rashmi paused and said, "I am dealing with something very serious, and I need your help."

"Go on."

Rashmi told him about the case right from the start, about how she reached from KD to Pigeon Delivery.

"That's a serious allegation," her uncle said, his face turning grim.

"It's not an allegation, just a hypothesis. I haven't come to any conclusion yet. In fact, to validate my hypothesis, I need your help to get me inside the organisation."

He let out a brooding hum. "I've to make a few phone calls. I'm sure you aren't planning to reveal your true identity to them."

"Of course."

"So I definitely can't quote my niece needs a job."

She nodded. "You truly are Dheeraj Purohit's brother."

He scowled at her playful remark. "Give me a few days and by a week or so you'll be sitting inside Pigeon Delivery's corporate office."

"Thanks a lot, uncle," Rashmi said with a genuine smile. She felt as if she hadn't smiled for ages. *No matter how far or how long you stay away from your loved ones, when you need them, they are always there for you.* "And I am sorry," Rashmi said, heaving a lungful of air. "After Papa left us, and then how Mumma"— she closed her eyes and looked away for a while – "I just felt too cut off from everyone. I began to hate everyone, every blood relation, every friend. I secluded myself from the whole world and just began to concentrate on my work. And then Pi Agency and my work pulled me away from everyone, and I let myself drift away."

"Why are you punishing yourself for what your mother did?" Purushottam asked sincerely. "Why so much hatred for everyone? Why so much hatred for her? She is your mother, after all."

"She was," Rashmi shot back. "She was my mother."

Purushottam sighed. "Look at me, I've moved on in my life. Why can't you?"

Her uncle, too, had a painful experience in relationships. She'd heard the news about his wife and daughter, but she never visited him to listen to his problem. Remorse filled her at the thought of it. She should've been with her uncle. He was all alone in the world, with pain and with agony.

"Your problem was different. You can move on. I cannot."

"Oh, come on. Don't behave like that college kid who thinks his break up story is the most painful story ever. Everyone's got some problem in their lives and everyone's got to live with it. And you've got to learn too. Move on.

Rashmi stood up. "I think I should leave now. I will be waiting for your call, uncle."

She began to walk toward the door when Purushottam said, "Why don't you leave that place, Rashmi. That house. Your Papa's house."

Rashmi turned back to Purushottam.

"That house will keep on reminding you of your past and those painful memories. Leave that place and start afresh."

"The one my father loved the most has already left him," Rashmi said, putting on her show of stoicism, pushing down the memories back into the dark caverns of her mind, the reflections which were forming a painful lump in her throat . "The other person he loved isn't going to repeat it."

Chapter 31

Pigeon Delivery's corporate office was situated at Rajendra Place in Central Delhi. It was a mere five kilometres west to Delhi's commercial hub, and literally, Delhi's heart—Connaught Place. Uncle Purushottam used his connections and arranged the interview at Pigeon Delivery for the next week. Malviya Nagar—where Rashmi's residence-cum-office was—wasn't directly connected to Rajendra Place by metro. Rashmi deemed driving as the better option. The travel time, anyway, would be the same.

Rajendra Place was a congregation of commercial buildings, each having its own name. Rashmi located Pragati Towers and took the elevator to the fifth floor. After reaching the fifth floor, she searched for the office, but couldn't locate it. She noticed a small board directing her to Pigeon Delivery office to the left.

There was a tinted glass door, through which Rashmi peeped inside. Inside was a small reception area, with a black reception desk topped with a glass. *My workstation.*

Pigeon Delivery had two vacancies available—receptionist and Kitchen staffer. It was easy for Rashmi to choose between the two.

On the front face of the reception desk was affixed a square panel of glass on which 'Pigeon Delivery' was printed in blue, along with the Twitter-like logo. There was no one sitting on the desk, which demonstrated the vacancy. To the left was another tinted glass wall, probably partitioning the main office from the reception.

The frosted glass door was locked. There was a switch on the left side with a bell symbol on it. Rashmi pushed the switch. Rashmi heard a girl's voice and she stepped back from the door.

As the door opened, Rashmi saw a girl in her mid-twenties wearing a denim shorts and talking to someone on the phone. Rashmi wondered if denim shorts were allowed in the office.

The girl gave her a vague nod, still on the call, and pointed with her chin toward a couch placed beside the reception desk. Rashmi entered and stood beside the couch.

"Okay, I have to go now," the girl said, and hung up the call. She looked at Rashmi and said, "Yes."

"I'm Malini Sharma," Rashmi said, offering her alias. "I came here for the receptionist's interview."

"Oh, yeah. Ankit told us this morning."

"Mr. Ankit Malik, right?" Rashmi asked.

"Yeah right," the girl said, showing little interest in Rashmi. She turned toward the second glass door, which was the entrance to the main office. "Come, Malini."

Rashmi entered the office. It was fairly large, twice the size of her basement office, and seemed like it could accommodate at least twenty people, though it didn't seem so from outside. There was another couch at one side of the entrance. Rashmi took her place on the couch. She began to scan the office with her eagle-eyes.

There were three long tables arranged in parallel along the length of the office with eight chairs on each side. She corrected her previous guess of seating capacity to forty-eight. Most of them were vacant. Rashmi estimated there were about thirty people. All the employees, be it males or females, were dressed casually. Some were sitting on the chairs, while some were casually lying on the beanbags with laptops on their laps. She could also spot an expensive-looking coffee machine kept at one corner, which her subordinates would always crave for. There was a fridge with a transparent door beside the machine. Through the transparent door, cans of soft drinks were visible. Focussing a bit more, she also noticed green bottles of Kingfisher Premium in the lowermost rack.

The start-up culture has gone too far, Rashmi thought. *I fear what would happen the day the investors came and saw where their investments are going.*

"Hi, Malini." A voice brought Rashmi out of her scanning mode. She saw Ankit Malik pacing toward her. He looked to be five and a half feet tall, his waist disproportionately wider than rest of his upper and lower body. He was in the same black polo from the footage, but untucked, probably to hide his flabby love handles. His short, sleek, neatly-combed hair stayed perfectly shaped, held by some kind of expensive hair product.

"Hello, sir," she said, noticing his round, double-chinned face and awkwardly long nose that looked similar to her own. Spots of previously prevalent pimples and acnes were apparent on his nose and cheeks.

Ankit shook her hand and said, "I think we don't need any boring formalities like an interview."

Rashmi shrugged. "Up to you, sir."

"Ah, don't call me sir. Ankit is fine. There's no 'sir' and 'ma'am' here."

"Okay" – Rashmi stopped herself from calling him 'sir' again – "Ankit."

"Sabrina," Ankit called across the office. A girl stood and came besides Ankit. "Meet Sabrina," Ankit said. "She is Russian, but she's been living in India for three years."

Sabrina's heart-shaped face had an ivory complexion, and her eyes sparkled green like emerald. Her blonde and silky hair parted from centre and streamed down until her bony shoulders. She was half a foot taller than Ankit, despite the flat shoes. She wore a tight-fitting, red dress, which ended at midthigh, revealing most of her voluptuous legs.

"Give her a brief intro about our work," Ankit instructed Sabrina, "introduce her to the guys here, and then explain her duties, though there isn't much to explain." He then turned to Rashmi. "And then you're good to go."

Chapter 32

"So, what exactly you do here?" Rashmi asked Sabrina. Rashmi had asked this question for the third time. The response from Sabrina for the previous two times was, "Entertainment."

It was Rashmi's third week in Pigeon Delivery. She got along well only with Sabrina. Other employees were just too busy to interact with her, except for requesting a few jobs like photocopying or scanning or shipping a courier. She didn't have much to do, either. Sabrina would occasionally give her data compilation jobs. Rashmi always tried to get useful data from those photocopies, and scanned the copied documents, but so far, she'd found nothing of use.

"I told you," Sabrina replied. "Entertainment."

"And what does that mean?"

"Leave it."

"No, you have to tell me today, what does this 'Entertainment' mean?" If Rashmi had to extract any useful information about Ankit Malik, she would need the help of an insider. And that insider could very well be Sabrina. And to use Sabrina for her cause, she had to befriend her. She needed to win her trust. So she threw this personal question again at her during lunch time.

Sabrina sighed . "When the amount of money a person gets doesn't commensurate with his age, he starts to squander it on superfluous things."

"Was that some Monday morning quote?"

Sabrina laughed. "You know how start-ups work. There is no fixed time to go back home, and work pressure is tremendous. There must be some form of entertainment for the male employees to reduce their frustration. Besides, who doesn't want an incentive in the form of a Russian girl?"

"No way," Rashmi said, abomination pouring inside her. Rashmi was more disgusted than shocked to know about Sabrina. She'd been hired by the company only because the guys here could fuck her whenever they wished to. She was no more than a—

"Whore," Sabrina said. It seemed she could read Rashmi's mind. "I am no more than a whore to them. And sometimes Ankit also uses me as a bait for the prospective investors."

"That's bad, Sabrina. That's really bad. I'm sure you don't like it, either."

"Like? I loathe myself, Malini. I came here to become a model. They said I would easily get a role in Bollywood. Music videos hunt for sexy blonde girls." She chuckled. "They called me sexy and that was enough for me. Such a fool I was…" she trailed off.

Rashmi, unlike her usual self, felt sorry for Sabrina. Alphalion or Ankit Malik wasn't just a drug dealer who was spoiling kids' lives, he was a human trafficker too. Whatever was happening to Sabrina was no less than human trafficking. She wished after all got over, she could help Sabrina, or at least get her a respectable job.

But she had a much bigger and serious problem to deal with now.

Chapter 33

It was ten minutes to nine when Rashmi entered her house and switched the lights on. She dropped her bag on the table beside the door and set her phone to charge. She saw the pile of articles stacked on the couch. She still hadn't been able to finish reading them.

She considered picking up the stack, but was too tired to do that.

She rubbed her eyes and leaned back. All her hopes, for now, were resting on Sabrina. Sabrina was not very happy with Ankit Malik. Rashmi just needed to push her to the point where Sabrina was ready to betray Ankit Malik. And when it happened, Rashmi would be ready to reveal her true identity to her.

She grabbed today's newspaper and read the headline on the first page. *Sunita Prabhakar Case: Delhi HC Asks Police to Expedite the Investigation.* Below the headline were the photographs of the late Sunita Prabhakar and her husband, Rishi Tanwar. *Everyone knows this bloody Tanwar is the killer,* Rashmi thought.

Rishi Tanwar was a politician and an ex-Member of Parliament. Two years ago, when he was an MP, his relationship with his wife was going through a rough patch, so much so that Sunita had left Tanwar's house and was living alone. Not long after, Sunita was found dead in her house. An autopsy had suggested suicide initially, but later revealed that the case was not as linear as it had seemed—the reports showed she had been poisoned. Almost a year after Sunita's demise, the police treated the case as a homicide. Since then, the investigation had been ongoing.

The newspaper couldn't hold Rashmi's attention. She folded it and tossed it back on the table. She imagined what would have been the scenario had this Sunita Prabhakar's case been handled by a private investigator.

But she was also aware of the truth that such things only happen in fiction. Such cases would seldom come to private detectives. Though there were some premium detective agencies in India which enjoyed high-profile clientele, Rashmi's Pi Agency was nowhere near that level. If she was to take her agency to such heights *someday,* she would have to solve Brajesh Arya's case. The success in this case wouldn't make her a famous detective overnight, but failure would surely hurt her goals. Losing wasn't an option.

Chapter 34

"What types of products does our company deliver?" Rashmi asked Sabrina.

Sabrina had just rushed outside the main office and put a bunch of papers stapled together in front of Rashmi. The sheets had the internship data of all the interns Pigeon Delivery had employed since last year. She'd had to compile the quarterly spend on interns. She picked through the papers slowly, making her disinterest and lethargy apparent to Sabrina. She was trying to get some information from Sabrina, but Sabrina was more interested in delegating the data compilation to her.

"We cater to all big e-commerce," Sabrina said.

"And what if I have to learn about the working of our company? Are there any procedure documents, or lists, or something which I can study?"

"Look, Malini, Ankit needs this sheet by tomorrow," Sabrina's coated her tone with a healthy warning. "You better focus the job at hand."

"Okay, I'll finish it in time, but what about my question?"

"The data can be accessed by our ERP. It is installed in the system of only those employees who are authorised to use it. You and I are certainly not, so don't think about it. Anyway, I don't believe a receptionist would benefit from learning about all that." Sabrina turned back to the main office.

"I never wanted to be a receptionist," Rashmi said, trying to stop Sabrina. "I don't want to be receptionist for all my life."

Sabrina stopped and turned. Her eyes reflected questions. Now Rashmi had to hit the soft spot in Sabrina's heart, in order to get what she aiming for. Rashmi leaned forward, as if trying to plead to Sabrina. "My sole purpose of joining this company was to learn so that I can work in the main office, like those guys sitting inside."

"It's not—I cannot help you. It's impossible," Sabrina walked inside the main office.

"Damn," Rashmi groaned.

*

Rashmi was sitting alone in a restaurant in a tower nearby. She saw Sabrina entering the outlet.

"You didn't order anything," Sabrina said.

"Nah. Waiting for you," Rashmi replied blankly.

Sabrina looked at her for a moment and said, "I can help you with what you said in the office."

A little hope sparked inside Rashmi.

"I'm on good terms with Shekhar, our IT guy. He can install the ERP on your system without questions."

"Thank you so much, Sab!" Rashmi just made up a nickname.

"No need for that." Sabrina waved her hand. "I just need to go out on a dinner date with him."

"Look, Sab. If you are uncomfortable doing this, then there is no need for it."

"It's okay. Everyone comes here to just earn money; you came here to learn. And if I play a little part in it, I'm more than grateful."

Chapter 35

The IT guy, Shekhar, installed the software on Rashmi's system. He gave her his user ID and password to access it. He was an admin, and with his login, Rashmi got access to all the modules of the ERP system.

"Thank you," Sabrina said cheerfully.

"Anything for you, baby," Shekhar responded with a malicious grin and returned to the office.

"Motherfucker," Sabrina mouthed, eyeing the office door.

"I don't know how did he agree" Rashmi said.

"Have to go on a movie date with him this weekend."

"I'm so sorry, Sab." Rashmi was genuinely sorry for her. This case was making her do horrible things.

"It's okay," Sabrina said. "Not a new thing for me. You carry on with the software."

When Sabrina left, Rashmi accessed the recent fulfilled orders. There were tons of them. She sorted the orders that had been meant for Rohan's college.

There were many orders, but she couldn't find out what was in the shipments. Logistics Companies would never know the items inside the packets. Moreover, Rashmi doubted if Pigeon Delivery would keep records of their illegal activities in the system. She searched, one by one, through all the menus and modules. She wasn't sure if she was really going to get anything fruitful out of the system, but from her experience, she knew investigation required data gathering. All data might not be of use, but to determine that, a PI had to gather the data in the first place.

She stumbled upon warehouse details for Pigeon Delivery. Diksha had told her that Pigeon Delivery had one warehouse in Udyog Vihar in Gurgaon, but when she checked in the system, it revealed two locations.

She pulled out her investigation notebook out of her bag and quickly noted down the address of second warehouses.

As she finished, Sabrina barged into the reception area. "Did you make the sheets I assigned you yesterday?"

"Fuck."

"Ankit will kill me," Sabrina said. "And you too."

*

Rashmi picked up the pile of paper and began to fill the data into Excel spreadsheets. As she finished first few pages, she realised that it was not an hour-long job as she'd expected it to be. She glanced at the clock—only twenty minutes left to the end of the day. *I've to hurry.*

Looking at the number of interns in the past one year, she noticed that company had more temporary employees than permanent ones. In fact, there were only a handful of employees, probably in single digits, that were permanent employees.

As she was working on the data, she came across a name—Karan Shukla, which sounded strangely familiar. She drew out the investigation notepad from her bag and turned the pages. Karan Shukla was the friend of Rohan whom she had questioned in the beginning of the case. She checked his records. He was with Pigeon Delivery during the first quarter of last year—from April to June.

She leaned back. *Karan Shukla has worked in a company which has delivered drugs to Rohan.* Was it a coincidence? *The primary tenet of sleuthing is when something has 'coincidence' written all over it, look carefully, it definitely isn't.* Her eyes shuffled between the computer screen and her notebook. *Either he knows nothing, or he knows everything.*

Chapter 36

Karan walked out of a coffee shop in Connaught place with a girl beside him. He shook hands with her. "Hope we meet again soon," he said, holding her soft hands.

The girl reciprocated with a smile. Her eyes dropped to her hand. "If you may, please."

"Oh, sorry," he said, pulling back his hand.

And they headed in opposite direction.

The affair with the Bhopal girl didn't last long, so Karan decided to find a local girl. Courtesy of Tinder, he found one soon. When he'd downloaded the app for the first time, his friends had said that downloading it was as good as guaranteeing getting laid on the first date, but he never got any such opportunity. He made a plenty of right swipes, hoping to find a match. He got a few matches as well. A few girls didn't respond. A few lazy ones responded, but made it clear they wanted to confine their relationship to WhatsApp chat.

After fancying his luck for a few weeks, he finally got a response from a girl to meet over coffee. From her Facebook profile, he came to know that she was a working professional in Gurgaon, indicating that she was certainly older than him. They arranged to meet at a coffee shop in Connaught place.

When he met the girl, he was a little disappointed as the girl didn't look as beautiful as in pictures. But then, he knew half a loaf was better than no bread. After a few minutes of awkwardness, the conversation went well. And after an hour, they decided to end their meeting for today. The girl didn't commit to meeting him again, but Karan was hopeful.

Karan now was heading toward Rajiv Chowk metro station gate number 6, which was nearest to N-Block. N-block was located at the outer circle of Connaught place, while the metro station gates were at the inner circle. There were a number of radial roads which connected the outer circle to the inner circle. As he took a radial road, he realised that he was on the wrong one, which was farther from the metro station. The one on the other side of the block should've dropped him straight on the metro station's entrance. Instead of going back, he took the middle alley which connected the two radial roads.

It was quarter to eight, and it had grown dark outside. The middle circle road was essentially a back-alley, deserted and dark.

He saw two silhouettes charging toward him. He moved to one side to let them pass. But to his surprise, he saw them shifting their path as well. When they neared him, he figured out one male and one female

Karan halted. "Excuse me."

The guy just smiled and looked over Karan's shoulder. Karan felt someone was standing behind him. He turned quickly and saw another woman. She was standing inches away from him. A small bulb hanging on the backside of a shop slightly revealed her face, and her face seemed familiar. In fact, he had met her a few weeks ago.

"Ms. Detective, right?" Karan said. He pointed his thumb toward the other two people. "Your friends, I guess."

"I have a question for you." Rashmi seemed to ignore him.

Karan held her breath.

"What do you know about Pigeon Delivery?" Rashmi asked.

Karan giggled. "Sounds like a weird service for pregnant pigeons?"

Rashmi grabbed him by his collar and slammed him against a vehicle parked beside them. "I'm in no mood to entertain your 'cool' jokes."

"I know nothing." Karan changed his tone immediately. His heart began to pound fiercely.

Rashmi tightened her grip on his collar.

From the corner of his eyes he saw a few people entering the street. "Help!" His voice barely made its way out of his throat owing to Rashmi's choking grip. He was surprised to see the skinny lady possessed such strength.

"Go on, call them. I will tell them that you were stalking this girl," Rashmi said, rolling her eyes toward her female colleague. "And then you can only imagine what people here at CP would do to you."

"No, please," Karan pleaded. "I will tell you everything."

"That's better."

"I was an intern there last year."

"I know that," Rashmi snapped, pressing him against the car door.

"They had asked me for an internship. When I joined, they asked me to get Brajesh Arya's son, Rohan, who was also my friend and classmate, into this drug thing. They somehow knew that we were into drugs."

"Why did they ask you to do so?"

"I don't know. I really, really don't know. They offered me an internship with a handsome stipend. That was enough for me to do whatever they asked for."

Rashmi released his neck. "So you used to buy from them?"

Karan gave a nod.

Rashmi put her hand on his shoulder and squeezed it. Her bony hand was heavier than it looked.

He glanced at her hand and gulped. "They sell drugs. But it's not available to everyone. It's for an elite group of people, the likes of Rohan."

"Then why didn't you tell me that when I met you for the first time?"

"These are dangerous people. What would I have done? And I also bought from KD, just once. So I didn't lie, either."

"You think you're smart," she spoke through gritted teeth.

"I am sorry, I am sorry," he squeaked.

"How do you buy from them?" The detective's questions didn't seem to end. He remained silent.

The detective pushed him again against the car, choking him again. "Wait, wait, I'm telling you," he implored. "They have a special WhatsApp number. A business account. Just send what you want, along with the quantity and your address. They will deliver at your doorstep."

"Give me that number," Rashmi hissed.

There was no point in denying that he didn't have the number. Rashmi would only make him suffer more. "It's in my phone," Karan groaned.

Rashmi released him from her clutches and allowed him to take out his mobile phone. Karan gasped for air and scrolled through the contacts quickly, then passed on the mobile phone as soon as he found the contact.

Her male colleague joined her and jotted down the number in a small notebook. "Where do they store all the drugs?" Rashmi asked.

"Some warehouse. I don't remember." He was still panting.

"The one which they have in Udyog Vihar?"

"No, not that one. It was a small one, somewhere in Delhi. I don't remember."

Rashmi looked at her employees, who were scribbling on his notebook.

Karan waited for a reply. There wasn't any. "Am I free to go?"

Rashmi returned his phone, scowling at him. "If anything you said turns out to be a lie—"

"It won't," Karan said. "Mark my words."

The detective and her team departed.

Ensuring that everyone was gone, Karan made a call. "I told her exactly what you instructed."

Chapter 37

"So, are we gonna order via Whatsapp?" Diksha asked, sipping Minute Maid and chewing the orange pulp. "And that's our evidence, right?"

From CP they returned to office. She enjoyed her outing today. Finally boss had involved her in some sleuthing work. And it turned out to be an easy one. She enjoyed how boss was mauling Karan Shukla. And how the meek guy had almost pissed in his pants.

"Not exactly," Rashmi said, swallowing down her espresso in a single gulp.

She tilted toward Akshay and whispered, "Vodka shot."

Akshay shushed her.

Diksha wondered how anyone could like espresso. *It has a bitter taste. It destroys the entire taste of your tongue. And the bitterness hangs around inside for hours.* She guessed that was the reason her boss's impudent behaviour.

"Before that," Rashmi said. "I need to check the second warehouse of Pigeon Delivery. It must be a storehouse or something. We need to have comprehensive evidence. We need to show the entire supply chain of the drugs as evidence—order fulfilment from source to customer. And then we'll submit the entire report with evidence to Mr. Arya."

"Speaking of vodka," Diksha whispered again, "Shall we go out tomorrow for a round of drinks?" It had been days she'd gone for clubbing. Her friends were busy off late. Rather she was less busy than them.

Akshay shushed her again.

*

Rashmi went to Okhla Industrial State the next day after work to have a look at the warehouse in question. The warehouse compound was enclosed by high walls, probably nine feet high, but from a distance, she could see that warehouse building was a small, single-storey, pre-fabricated structure. It seemed like a temporary structure, perfect for the purpose it was supposed to be served. The compound was also smaller compared to the other buildings in the vicinity.

The compound was unguarded, save for a tall gate. She sneaked through the gate. There was no movement inside, but the lights inside were on. She came back inside her car and waited.

She waited for hours. It was only at eleven in the night she saw the lights going off. After a few minutes, a man came outside on his bike and left.

Chapter 38

"What do we store at Okhla warehouse?" Rashmi asked.

It was after office hours, and Rashmi and Sabrina were having dinner together. In fact, Rashmi had planned for this dinner so that she could pull information from Sabrina.

Sabrina sipped the sangria. "How did you know about it? Oh, right. From the ERP."

Rashmi nodded weakly.

She finished chewing the apple slices and said, "It's none of your business."

Rashmi beamed. "I heard Pigeon Delivery sell some 'special things' from there."

Sabrina put down the wine glass. It was her third drink and emerald green eyes had gone heavy. "Listen, I didn't give you the access to ERP for this."

"I didn't learn it from the ERP," Rashmi defended. "A friend told me."

"What?"

"He heard guys these days get drugs from Pigeon Delivery."

Sabrina looked around cautiously and gestured Rashmi to lower her voice. "Malini, have you gone mad?" she whispered, leaning forward. "This is illegal."

"So it's right?" Rashmi said.

Sabrina leaned back. Her silence was as good as a nod for Rashmi. She waved at a waiter for another glass of sangria.

"It was all Ankit's idea," Sabrina said. "He had left his high-profile banking job and started this logistics business with great enthusiasm. But it didn't seem to grow as much as he had intended. He wasn't getting investors, either."

Rashmi was aware of how start-ups in India were falling on their faces, even after being embarked on with much enthusiasm and passion. The sole reason, she believed, was lack of innovation. The MBAs-turned-entrepreneurs of India were just plainly picking the successful global business models, adjusting them as per local needs, and implementing them the same way. Countries like China, Japan, and South Korea were far ahead of India in terms of filing patents.

"So he came up with this new drug business model," Sabrina continued. "He tied up with the dealers. He tapped the potential customers using peddlers' connections. He now wants to establish a monopoly on the drug business in Delhi." Her new wine glass arrived, and she took a swig.

"Can I get drugs if I walk into the warehouse and tell them that I work for Pigeon Delivery?" Rashmi asked.

"Are you mad?" Sabrina exploded. "That warehouse guy would contact Ankit if you go there, and Ankit will fuck you, literally." Her voice was buoyant now, and her words were coming out unfiltered. "Like he fucks me. Not everyone in the company knows about this illicit business. He doesn't want everyone to know about this aspect of Pigeon Delivery. And a receptionist? Who the fuck are you?" Sabrina stroked her forehead. "Damn this wine." She took a large gulp. "And I didn't know you take drugs."

"It's not for me. For a friend."

"I know, I know."

"No, I seriously don't do drugs."

Sabrina looked busy savouring her wine. "I'm not judging you, Malini."

"I need your help," Rashmi said. "I am going to that warehouse. Ask for some sachets of cocaine. And I will say Ankit has told me to do so. I will ask the warehouse guy to call you and confirm."

She put her glass back. "Fuck you, Malini. You are going way overboard now. I am not going to do this. It's suicide."

"I will handle it, don't worry. I am not going to get you in trouble."

"You are such a bitch," Sabrina said, finishing her drink. "Ankit will kill you."

Rashmi just smiled, cursing Sabrina internally. This case was really making her do terrible things.

"I will have something harder now," Sabrina winked, curling her fingers, save for the middle one. "I mean a harder drink." She cracked up, opening her all fingers.

Rashmi laughed, too, continuing to curse her beneath her laughter.

Chapter 39

Rashmi arrived at the warehouse the next day. When she was about to reach the warehouse, she had instructed Akshay to place the order on WhatsApp to be delivered to the office address. She also asked him to stay back at the office to receive the order. She switched on the spy camera hidden strategically inside her bag. The unguarded wicket gate was unbolted, and Rashmi entered through it. She had already received the confirmation from Akshay about a weed order placement.

The compound seemed deserted. It was six in the evening, and it was desolate, as she had expected. A bike that she saw yesterday was parked inside.

The only entrance to the shed was a rolling shutter door, painted in the same blue as of the Pigeon Delivery logo.

She entered the building. She was relieved to find a man sitting just across a table placed next to the door.

"Hello," the man called, not with a greeting tone, but with a questioning one. "What do you want?"

"I am from Pigeon Delivery."

"So?" the man asked, apparently not impressed.

"You must have received an order a little while ago," Rashmi said, and told him the mobile number from which Akshay had texted. She spoke loudly, ensuring that the video recorder would catch her voice clearly.

The man took out his mobile phone and checked it. "Yes, but what do you want?"

"This one's a special order for a special client and I am responsible for its timely dispatch—that is now."

The man arched one brow. "No one's ever come directly from Pigeon Delivery for any order."

"As I told, this one is a special order. You may contact Ankit Malik's assistant, Sabrina."

"Why don't I call Malik himself?" the man said, tapping the screen of his phone.

Rashmi's heartbeat sped up, but she kept calm and said, "Ankit Malik is attending an important meeting and wouldn't like to be disturbed. If you still want to disturb him, you may go ahead."

The man stared at Rashmi for a while and inserted his mobile phone back inside his shirt pocket. "Come."

Rashmi smiled softly. *There's a fine line between intimidation and deterrence.*

Rashmi realised that most of the compound was empty. But she could see that the rectangular patches were darker and cleaner than rest of the flooring, like her house's wallpaper. Which meant something was removed from here recently. Today?

The man took her to a small room where plastic bins were stacked. Rashmi found bins similar to the ones kept outside dairy outlets, inside which milk pouches were stored. The man inserted his hand inside one bin, which was kept at a height above his head, and drew out a small pouch. "I will call the delivery guy. He'll take this out for delivery in a while," the man said, and walked out, calling someone on the phone.

Rashmi stayed back and picked up the bin from which the man had taken out the pouch. The bin was empty. She pulled down a few more bins one by one. All were empty.

"Trouble finding something?"

Rashmi whirled as she heard the voice.

Hands crossed and leaning against one of the edges of door, with a sly smile on his acne-filled face, was Ankit Malik.

Chapter 40

It was a lazy post-lunch period. Akshay's boss, Rashmi, was at the Pigeon Delivery office. Over the past few weeks, he hadn't been involved in the case. There was practically nothing to do. He would scan KD's laptop and would write down any observation he would make for boss.

"What do you do on KD's laptop?" Diksha asked.

"Unlike you I'm a detective. I don't just have digital marketing to do here. I've to look for evidence, find clues, and decode riddles."

Diksha threw him an odd look. "KD's laptop has only two folders and I know what's in there. So don't fool me."

"Oh, shut up. If I do really want porn there's Google for that."

However, Akshay would accept that KD did have a good collection of porn. He wasn't getting an opportunity to insert his flash drive into KD's laptop and get hold of the collection.

He rifled through the files for further twenty minutes when sleep began to engulf him. He nodded off for a moment and woke up in a flash. He looked at Diksha, embarrassed, to check if she'd noticed him.

"You can sleep on the table," Diksha said, not looking at him. "I won't tell boss."

"No, I wasn't sleeping. It was just—" He had no justification.

"Any idea when she is coming back?" Diksha asked.

"No, she probably isn't coming to office today, either."

Diksha giggled. "I think she has started to love her new job."

Akshay rubbed his eyes and stood up. He went inside the bathroom and splashed water on his face. When he returned, he saw Diksha looking at him with a sly smile. "What?" he asked.

"Let's go out," she said with her usual excitement. "Select city walk?"

Akshay knew that the primary reason for any girl to go to a shopping mall was shopping. He didn't want to fool around in the mall aimlessly for hours.

"Boss might come anytime. You know she never tells us anything."

"She isn't coming, yaar." Diksha waved her hand. "Have you seen her in the office for weeks?"

Akshay considered it was better not to respond.

Diksha showed her phone to her. "Have you ever been to Cyber Hub?"

"My friends in Gurgaon say a lot about it, but I've never been there."

She scrolled on her phone. "Look this pub is offering Happy Hours before five. It's quarter to four now. If we hurry, we can make it to Cyber Hub before five.

"Have you gone out of your mind? I'm not going anywhere." Akshay got back to KD's laptop. He realised it had been months since he'd had beer. Akshay believed that if men were asked privately, promised to keep their answers confidential, which they loved more—beer or their spouse? They would surely pick beer. His mind filled with the image of beer mugs filled with golden liquid, bubbles rising from base and mingling with the thick froth topping the mug.

"What do you say?" Diksha asked, her eyes twinkling with excitement. "You won't get this opportunity again."

Akshay shook his head.

"Come on, it's Friday night."

He shut the lid of the laptop.

*

They took a stroll to Diksha's PG. She wanted to change before they head for Cyber Hub. "What's the problem with these clothes?" he'd asked her.

She didn't answer. But he knew the answer. Girls loved to wear a new attire everytime they go out. They search for opportunities to try different clothing, shoes, jewellery. Sometimes, they didn't even repeat the attire for months.

"Book an Uber for us," she said, waking inside the PG, "I'll come back in a while."

Her definition of 'a while' was twenty minutes.

When she walked out of the entrance, Akshay took a few seconds to realise she was Diksha. She wore a black velvet crop top and a pink skirt which hugged her wasp waist and flared down, ending well above her knees. He remembered he'd gifted his ex, Smriti, a similar pink skirt. Her hair looked more voluminous now, and wavier at the ends.

"Let's go," she said. "We're running late."

The Uber had arrived five minutes earlier. When he sat beside her, he noticed for the first time that she'd muddy brown eyes. He'd never thought that he would find Diksha beautiful someday.

When they entered the pub of Diksha's choice, it was bustling with people. "Whoa," Diksha said. "I didn't know this place is full at this hour."

"It's Friday ma'am," a staff said, offering them a seat by the bar. "All the office get togethers are planned mostly on Fridays."

Akshay noticed most of the patrons were in formals, lanyard with their IDs hanging around their necks. He wished if they'd their office in such a place. *Someday*, he thought.

The waiter arrived with a pitcher of Belgian wheat and poured in their mugs. They chinked their mugs. Akshay pulled a long sip. "Must be a new thing for you," Akshay said, showing the mug. "Gujarat is a dry state."

"Very funny." Diksha made a face and quaffed the drink.

Akshay finished the first mug quickly. He felt a little tipsy; the beer had started to affect his brain. By the time he finished the second, his mind was spinning. Diksha was still in her first drink. When poured his third drink into his mug, the beer foamed and erupted out of the mug. "Oops." He moved the mug away from him, the foam still spilling out and forming a pool on the table. "Don't think I'm drunk."

Diksha laughed. "I can see. You're done in only two mugs? So weak."

"Nothing like that." Akshay leaned back, leaning back on his wooden bar stool. "It's because I am drinking after a while." When he closed his eyes, Smriti's face flashed in his mind.

Chapter 41

Diksha was amused by Akshay's behaviour. Usually, it was Akshay who had to bear her antics, but today, it was the other way around.

He had consumed three mugs of beer by now, and Diksha was now getting worried. It would be a daunting task to handle a guy half a foot taller than her and bit muscular, out of his senses, and swinging and swaying. She didn't even know where Akshay lived. She wasn't expecting Akshay to get drunk so easily.

"Arora." She shook him.

He opened his eyes. "No, I'm not drunk."

"Have I said that you're drunk?"

"I was just thinking about..." he paused. "Nothing." He gulped down his fourth drink.

"Easy, Arora. It's only six. We've got time."

Akshay gawked at her. "You look like her. And now you speak like her."

"Her? Whom are you talking about?"

"Nothing." Akshay turned his face away.

"Are you kidding me, Arora."

"So what do I do," his voice rose. "I still remember her, man."

The giggle had almost come out, but Diksha caught it in her throat. It wasn't too difficult for her to figure out Akshay was remembering his lost love. Guys would often do that after drinking, and it was funny.

"You think it's funny," Arora said, locking his heavy eyes on her. He must have caught her smiling.

"No, it's not funny, but why did you say I look like her?"

"Because you look like her. Whenever I see you, I remember Smriti."

"Smriti, your girlfriend?"

He nodded. "Ex-girlfriend."

She stifled a giggle again. "Why did you guys fall out?"

"She left me."

"And may I know why?"

"She wanted more from me. Something for which I wasn't ready."

Diksha understood why did their relationship break. It happened quite often with couples. Guys weren't ready for a serious relationship and girls wanted a firm commitment.

"How could I have told her that I was going to marry her," Akshay slurred, "when even I didn't know if I was ready to spend my whole life with her?"

"But she wasn't wrong, either."

"Yeah, why not? You're a girl plus you look like her, you're surely gonna support her."

Diksha chuckled. "I'm not favouring her, but that was what she wanted out of a relationship. When she found you didn't have it for her, she left you. What was the point in dragging the relationship which had no future?"

"She fucking left me for some other guy," Akshay spat. "He's dating someone."

Diksha shrugged. "May be that guy was ready to marry her."

Akshay leaned back, crossing his arms. "No point in talking to you. You won't understand."

She wasn't actually qualified to have the talks on relationships. She had never been to one. She had plenty of friends, some of them were close ones, but she never felt the need to get into a relationship. She never understood what special you felt about someone that you made him your boyfriend. "Okay, let's assume she comes back to you. Would you be able to assure her that you would marry her?"

Akshay's eyes never left the empty beer mug. Diksha hadn't noticed when he'd gulped down the fifth one.

"See, you're still not ready," Diksha said. "Let her go, Arora," she softened her tone. "You deserve someone better. She deserves someone better, too. It's just you both don't deserve each other."

He covered his face with his hands.

"As for my looks, sorry I can't change it." She winked. "So you've to bear with my face as long as we are together."

Akshay let out a soft chuckle. "No, you're beautiful." He leaned back, his head now facing the ceiling. "You really are very beautiful." His eyes were now closed.

Diksha feared if Akshay slept here, it would become impossible to take him back home. She was about to call the waited for bill when she saw Akshay's cell lit up, buzzing on the wooden bar table. She leaned forward and saw the caller's ID: Boss

Fuck. "Akshay," she called out loud.

"What?" Akshay said, eyes still closed.

"Boss is calling," she said with urgency in her tone.

"Hmm…" It seemed Akshay wasn't listening.

She stood climbed down the high bar stool and walked beside him, grabbed his shoulders and shook them. "Akshay, Boss is calling you."

Akshay opened his eyes wide and bolted upright. "Where… what?"

"Boss is calling," Diksha shrieked.

Akshay grabbed his cell phone and answered the call. "Yes, Boss." He listened. "Yes…okay. I will do it." It seemed he wasn't drunk at all.

Though Diksha was worried to see her boss calling, she couldn't hold her laughter back at seeing how Akshay regained his attentiveness. Akshay gestured her to stay silent.

"What happened?" Diksha asked.

"You got us fucked," Akshay said, running his fingers through his hair. "Boss just told me to order weed via WhatsApp to the office address, the number which Karan gave us."

"What's the big deal? Give me your phone; I will order it."

"And asked us to stay at the office. She is going to the warehouse and will get the packet dispatched. The delivery guy will reach the office address within an hour."

"Now, that is a problem. We have to get moving now."

Akshay held his forehead, seemed to struggle with the dizziness. "That's not all. Boss has called Brajesh Arya to the office."

*

Diksha and Akshay took an Uber cab from Gurgaon for Malviya Nagar. It was peak rush hour, and the traffic on Mehrauli-Gurgaon road was moving at a snail's pace. Forty-five minutes had passed, and they still hadn't reached the halfway mark. She peeked out of window. She could only see a sea of twinkling red tail lights. "We're dead," she murmured.

"I am feeling nauseous," Akshay gasped.

"Sir," the cab driver said in a worried voice, "don't puke inside my car. I won't be able to take more rides today."

Diksha saw a metro station a hundred meters away. *"Bhaiya,"* she said to the driver, "Drop us here."

"What happened?" Akshay asked, rubbing his chest.

"We have to catch the metro to reach it in time."

Chapter 42

"Ms Malini Sharma," Ankit said as he stepped casually inside the store room, "you could have taken a better name. I don't like this name."

Rashmi stood her ground.

Ankit grinned. "Rashmi Purohit would have been a better name, right?"

Four heavyset men entered the storehouse and surrounded Rashmi.

"What did you think, Ms Detective?" Ankit said. "I didn't know who you really are? I knew even before you joined my company."

The bulky creatures inched toward Rashmi, stretching their necks and cracking knuckles.

Rashmi understood that she was busted. There were several questions ringing inside her mind, but she focussed her thoughts toward escaping first. She quickly glanced at the attackers. *Bulky. Powerful. Sluggish.*

She knew if she tried to run, the goons would attack her and catch her. She ducked. The bulky goons took time to bend downward. She plunged from the gap between the two men and got up behind them. She grabbed the head of one of the men from behind, squeezing his eyes.

The man screamed in agony.

She pulled the man backward, banging his head on the ground.

A meaty arm wrapped around her neck. She could smell sweat from the man's armpit. She bit his arm. It felt like a rhino's skin. She dug her tooth deep.

The man yelled and his grip loosened.

A third man charged toward her.

She stepped on the belly of the fallen man and jumped in the air, swinging her right leg, and kicking his head with all the power she had.

Second body hit the ground.

The man who'd grabbed her shouldered her on her back. She stumbled forward. The fourth man blocked her motion by kicking her on her stomach.

Air sucked out of his lung as she fell on the stack of empty bins. The stack fell like a pack of cards.

She grabbed two empty bins on her hands and sandwiched the fourth man's head between the bins. The man clutched his skull and sat on the floor. She then swung around and hit the last man's head. The man just stumbled backward.

Rashmi checked on the other three men, who were getting back up. She couldn't keep on fighting with them. She barrelled into the last man standing, pushing him against the wall and jamming her knee into his crotch.

The last man held his balls, and crumpled on the floor.

Ankit Malik blocked the door. Fear had gripped his face.

Rashmi closed her fists and charged at him.

"Don't hit me," he cried, crouching on the floor and covering his head with his hands.

Rashmi ignored him bolted for the exit.

She staggered forward, and after a heartbeat, her mind registered the pain at the back of her head. She dropped on her knees. Her mind spun.

Everything seemed to black out. She raised her head and saw a woman, blonde hair, holding a thick stick, and a menacing smile on her face.

"Sabrina," Rashmi mumbled as her world faded to black.

Chapter 43

"Akshay, let's go." Diksha shook Akshay, who was slowly losing himself in a slumber.

"I…I can't," Akshay stuttered. "I can't walk. I am feeling sick. I'll throw up."

Diksha grabbed Akshay's wrist and pulled him out of the car. She ploughed through the crowd, dragging Akshay behind her. Akshay was stumbling and swinging behind her, pausing in between, and making faces as if he might puke up any moment.

It took her another half an hour of embarrassment to drag her sloshed co-worker to the office. The delivery guy hadn't called Akshay yet, so Diksha assumed they weren't too late.

Rashmi's house was dark; not a single light on. She stepped down to the basement, holding Akshay along, and drew out office keys from her purse. She put the key into the slot and turned it right. The key didn't turn. The door was not locked.

Shit. She feared they had forgotten to lock the door. But she remembered Akshay had locked the door and given the keys to her. *Then how is it open?*

As the door opened, Akshay darted inside the washroom. Diksha switched the light buttons on, but the lights didn't flicker. *Power outage?* she thought. *But we have a backup here.*

She switched on her cell phone's flashlight to check the backup generator. She suspected that the generator wasn't functioning. She lit up the flashlight and threw it toward the washroom. She didn't sense any movement inside. She wondered Akshay had fallen asleep inside the washroom.

She turned toward the generator, but collided with someone.

"Akshay!" Diksha yelped. Akshay, however, seemed awkwardly beefy. She spilled the torchlight at his face and realised it wasn't Akshay. She stepped back quickly. "Who are you?"

"Delivery boy, ma'am."

Diksha noticed his accent was foreign and strange, and that he was wearing a cap.

"From Pigeon Delivery?" Diksha asked.

The guy nodded. Diksha waited for the guy to produce the package, but he didn't. He blankly stared back at Diksha. When she looked closely, she realised his face was covered with a balaclava, the eyes and mouth being the only parts of the face peeking out.

She heard footsteps on the stairs. She glanced over the burly man's shoulder. An awkwardly tall figure, probably seven feet, entered the office. Something was seriously wrong here.

The guy glanced back as the other man entered and turned back toward Diksha. "We brought your delivery, ma'am. Your death!" he said in Hindi. His accent sounded like that popular African guy from YouTube who sang Bollywood songs, and sometimes Punjabi and Bhojpuri, too.

He grabbed Diksha's neck and pushed her back.

The phone dropped from Diksha's hand, and she fell onto the floor. "Akshay," Diksha yelled, hoping Akshay hadn't passed out inside the washroom.

The cell phone fell on its screen, flashlight up, illuminating the office slightly.

The African-Hindi accented guy said to the tall man, "I don't want to get my hands dirty on Indian soil."

The tall man loomed over her, a rope dangling in his hand. He looked gigantic. Diksha got up and ran, but felt a sharp pain in her head as the tall guy pulled her by the hair. She shrieked, and the men laughed.

The man wrapped the rope around Diksha's neck and started choking her. She tried to wriggle her fingers between the rope and her neck, hoping to loosen the grip, but the man's strength was too much for her. She tried to cry out so that Akshay, or someone from outside, could hear her voice. She put all her strength to shake her body free, but nothing was working for her.

"Take these laptops," the seven-footer said. "We have to make it look like a burglary."

In the midst of this struggle, the washroom door opened. Akshay hobbled out . His right hand was on the door's edge, and left on his stomach. "I felt like I would throw up," Akshay said, "but nothing happened."

The African accented guy blurted out, "Tu *Ladki sambhal, main ise dekhta hu.*" Take care of the girl—I'm going after the guy.

A fraction of a second distraction made the tall man to lose his grip. Diksha pushed the guy's hands away and ducked, leaving the rope hanging in the air.

Chapter 44

Akshay stepped out of the washroom, his mind spinning and stomach heaving. The world outside was dark and dancing. As he narrowed his vision, he was taken aback seeing two intruders. One of them, a towering, lanky fellow, was choking Diksha on the floor. The second intruder, a gorilla-like man, hurled toward him.

Akshay was close to the exit door and could run away easily, but he couldn't leave Diksha in the mouth of danger. He had to stay there and save Diksha. But first, he had to save himself, which seemed a daunting task at the moment.

Akshay stepped back, his reaction time feeling slow. A heavy blow landed on his face. He fell flat on the floor and registered the pain after a few seconds. The pain receptors, too, were lagging. The big guy clutched Akshay's neck between his thick, muscular arms. He was now also trapped, like Diksha.

In the faint flashlight of Diksha's mobile phone, he saw Diksha quickly escaping the tall guy's trap. She slithered across the floor and extended her hands, trying to grab something—it was her bag. It seemed like a desperate measure. Her bag was definitely not capable of stopping her attacker. She was still lying on the ground and digging through the purse.

"Run away," Akshay bawled.

Diksha didn't seem to listen, and kept rummaging. The tall guy came behind her and stamped on her legs. "I love these heels," he said.

Diksha screamed in agony.

"Don't hurt her, please," Akshay wailed.

The tall figure guffawed. As he bent down, Diksha whirled, as if she was waiting for him to reach her. She pulled her hand out of the bag. She had clutched an object, which appeared to be a deodorant tube. She sprayed the content on the man's eyes.

"Take that, fucker." Diksha emptied it. This time, the man screamed in agony.

Pepper spray, Akshay thought. "Beat the shit out of him, girl."

Diksha picked the laptop from the table and smashed it into his face. He prayed it wasn't his boss's laptop.

Judging by the cries of the man, it seemed she was beating the shit out of him. The hefty man, seeing his companion getting thrashed, hurled Akshay away and went for Diksha. Akshay barely managed to keep himself from falling on the floor. He ran forward and grabbed him from behind, wrapping his arms around the attacker's waist. He was able to stop the intruder, but couldn't stop his own motion. It was too late when he realised that he had to stop; his body hit the colossal structure from behind. He imagined his pose—grabbing a guy's waist, practically spooning—and felt a rush of embarrassment.

What's the use of all those bench presses and deadlifts? he challenged himself. He pushed the attacker's body onto the ground. He fought his drunkenness and climbed on the mountainous body before the big guy could get up.

The big guy punched Akshay's ribs on both sides, his fists landing on his ribs like hammer blows.

Akshay held his breath. *Engage your core. Engage your core.* He told himself, as he would do before doing two-hundred pounds squats.

Despite being hurt, Akshay maintained his hold. Diksha, too, joined Akshay and started kicking the big guy without stopping.

The punches were now hurting Akshay's ribs and stomach. His stomach churned. This time, it felt like his stomach wouldn't endure anymore.

And it gave up.

The contents of his stomach flowed out of his mouth and splashed on the big guy's wide chest.

Diksha screamed in disgust—followed by the hulk.

Chapter 45

Rashmi's world reappeared as she opened her eyes. Slowly, she felt the pain in the back of her neck, which grew intense. She saw the chubby Ankit Malik with his ugly smile standing in front of her. On his side was Sabrina, holding Rashmi's bag, inside which Rashmi had hidden her spy camera. Ankit's hand was wrapped around Sabrina's waist, caressing her waist and sometimes moving down to her ass. The four goons stood around her, their expressions suggesting that they were dying to take revenge on Rashmi.

"A few smooth talks with my assistant and you thought you could buy her loyalty," Ankit said, maintaining the same repulsive smile.

Sabrina drew out the spy camera from the bag and showed it to Rashmi. Her lips curved into an evil smile.

Ankit rolled his eyes toward Sabrina and looked back at Rashmi. "I knew you had taken Brajesh Arya's case right from the day he showed up at our office."

Rashmi fought through the pain to understand what Ankit was saying.

"Why did you think we gave you the interns list?" Ankit continued. "Because we wanted you to find Karan Shukla's name on it."

Rashmi now began to understand. Karan Shukla would have informed Ankit Malik the day she had interviewed him for the first time.

Sabrina dropped the spy camera on the floor.

"Do you really think you can order drugs on WhatsApp and we'll deliver them to your doorstep?" Ankit let out a derisive chuckle as he crushed the spy camera under his foot. "Do you think Alphalion would leave so many loose ends?"

Ankit called Alphalion in third person. That made Rashmi wonder if he really was Alphalion, or it was her one of the many errors of judgement.

Ankit glanced at his goons, and the goons understood what they had to do. Two goons came near Rashmi with a bundle of thick rope and tape in their hand. One of them wrapped the rope around Rashmi's arms and tied her to the chair on which she was sitting. She struggled to avoid being tied up, shaking her body, but realised that her legs were already tied by the rope. The man who tied her from the chair now ripped a portion of the tape and pasted it over Rashmi's mouth. Then he brought her hands forward and tied both wrists together.

Her body was now locked to the chair. She stopped wriggling. The goons left the storeroom, while Ankit and Sabrina were still there.

Rashmi looked at Sabrina and furrowed her brow in fury.

Sabrina smiled. "What? I told you I was a whore."

Don't insult whores.

Ankit pulled Sabrina closer, his hand gently but unsparingly holding onto her waist. "Poor lady thought 'Sab' has become her best friend."

"Oh, is that so?" Sabrina gave her mocking puppy eyes.

The goons re-entered the storeroom carrying canisters. They start pouring out a liquid on the floor, spreading it around the entire room. She identified the smell— kerosene.

"Goodbye, Ms Detective." Ankit said and walked out of the room, his fat ass swaying like one of those pirate-ship rides in amusement parks.

Sabrina blew a kiss to Rashmi and followed him. The expressionless goons were the last ones to leave.

After a minute or so, Rashmi heard a chattering sound. She could easily recognize it; it was the sound of burning flames. Yellow reflections were visible on the walls now. The fire reached the warehouse in the next few seconds, and covered the storage room in no time.

Rashmi was soon surrounded by the flames, dancing around her like witches, waiting to engulf her flesh and bones.

Chapter 46

Akshay gathered his senses back and tried to interpret his surroundings. He saw a blurred image of a masked man lying beneath him. He remembered vomiting all over him. *This has to be the most embarrassing thing I have ever done.*

"You fucker," the big guy roared.

Akshay felt as if he'd woken from a deep slumber. The intruder rolled on one side, pushing Akshay away. He stood up quickly, removed his T-shirt, and threw it away, revealing his swarthy upper body. His enormous belly hung out.

"Bastard." His clenched teeth shone pale in the flashlight's illumination. He seized Akshay's hair and lifted him.

Akshay wasn't left with much energy to fight back. He held his attacker's fist, trying escape.

Diksha ran up from behind and grabbed the big guy's thick arm. "Leave him." It barely affected him. He swung his arm, shooing her away like a fly.

Akshay surrendered, closing his eyes, waiting for first of the several blows coming.

But before it could happen, he heard footsteps on the stairs. The silhouettes of a man and two other seemingly huge people appeared at the door. "Excuse me," said a voice as he walked forward, "is this Ms Rashmi Purohit's office?" He came in the illuminating zone of the flashlight. "I am Brajesh Arya."

Confusion spread across Brajesh Arya's face at seeing the office dark. But the confusion soon gave way to shock. Akshay understood the reason for this shock—it was not normal to see a half-naked man clutching the hair of another guy, like those WWE fights. The bouncers accompanying Brajesh Arya seemed to be his personal bodyguards.

Akshay felt someone running across the room. It was the seven-footer, who was now fully conscious. The tall guy ran past Mr. Arya and up the stairs. The bodyguards' heads turned, without trying to catch or stop him.

"Run, man," the tall guy's voice echoed in the staircase. "You don't want to get into a police case in this country."

The half-naked man left Akshay's hair alone and darted toward the exit. One of the bodyguards stretched his hands and grabbed him. His hand, however, slipped against the big guy's sweaty body.

Yuck! Akshay thought, realising the bodyguard's hand could have touched his vomit, too.

Brajesh Arya gaze shuffled between the fleeing men and Akshay. His bodyguard ran outside to catch both the intruders. "What the hell was happening here?" Brajesh Arya asked, placing his hands on his waist.

His bodyguards returned. "They are gone."

Brajesh Arya was still staring Akshay and Diksha, waiting for an answer.

"You saved our lives, sir." Akshay got up, panting. "And you may take a cut from our payment as compensation."

Chapter 47

apa, he will die," nine-year-old Rashmi said. She was watching a magic show on television with her father. Dheeraj Purohit's family were supposed to watch TV for half an hour every day after dinner. Her mother, however, would remain busy, doing dishes and preparing for the next morning's meal.

"He will not, beta," Dheeraj said, caressing Rashmi's chin length hair.

The magician had been tied up with a rope and put inside a trunk. The trunk was locked from outside, and it was going to be dropped in a lake.

Rashmi kept her eyes locked on the screen, without so much as blinking. The trunk was hanging from a crane, which was lowering it into a lake. The trunk submerged completely inside the water. The water stopped rippling.

Rashmi was watching eagerly, and so was the audience surrounding the lake. Rashmi was praying for the well-being of the magician. She had hydrophobia, and a sight of a man locked inside a submerged trunk chilled her to the core.

The camera panned slightly away from the dropping point and zoomed out. The magician magically emerged from the lake. He raised his hands and waved them toward the audience. The crowd roared, cheered, and clapped for him, and so did Rashmi. It was indeed magic for her.

But as she grew, she came to know that there wasn't anything magical in what that magician had done, or any magic, for that matter. All magic was nothing but tricks backed up by skill and science. Out of curiosity, and when she learned about Google and YouTube, she learnt how the magician had performed the escape tricks.

In the midst of the dancing flames, drenched in her own sweat, Rashmi sat tied on the chair, remembering her past. Her father's memory caught her mind for a moment, and she sat on the chair like a corpse. She pulled herself back from the memories as the heat grew severe.

She had learnt from the magic trick analysis that magicians would expand their bodies and tense their muscles when they were tied by the ropes. After they disappeared from the eyes of the audience, they relaxed their muscles, loosening the rope.

She had also learnt how magicians managed to untie their tied wrists—a simple modification in the position of the wrists when they were being tied. When her wrists were being tied together, she had rotated her wrists outward from the bottom, thereby creating an inverted 'V' shaped gap between her wrists. She rotated her wrists back, loosening the rope's grip. She twisted her hands a few times and got them out. In next sixty seconds, she freed herself of the rope.

Chapter 48

Rashmi took an Uber from the warehouse to her office. Her hair was untied and frizzled, and her face darkened with smudged soot. The driver looked hesitant when she entered the car, but then, it was none of his business.

After what had happened, she was extremely tensed about her two subordinates. She was on the verge of dying, and had somehow managed to pull things out of the fire—literally. How would those kids manage to do the same if, unfortunately, they had to face the same situation?

It took her an hour to reach the office. As the cab arrived in front of the office, she hoped out of the car and darted towards the office. From the stairs, she could see the lights of the office were on. But she couldn't hear any voices.

She barged into the office. In front of the office desk, she saw Akshay sitting on a chair, his elbows propped on his knees and his face covered by his hands. Diksha was sitting beside him.

"Ms Purohit."

She heard a voice and turned toward the right corner of the office. Brajesh Arya was sitting on her chair, in front of the white board, in front of his son's name. Behind him were standing two bouncer-like men.

Akshay and Diksha, too, looked toward the door when they heard Brajesh Arya's voice, becoming attentive and standing up as they saw their boss.

The office reeked of vomit. She observed a small area on the floor wet and wiped off.

"I think you owe me a lot of explanations, Ms Purohit," Brajesh Arya said as he stood up.

Rashmi closed her eyes for a second. The past few hours had been the most chaotic time of her life. To top it, she had absolutely no idea what had happened behind her. She had almost forgotten that she'd called Brajesh Arya to her office, which she now felt was a stupid decision. *I've already made a lot of stupid decisions in this case, anyway.* "Yes." That was she could all say.

"I had expected you to be a lot better. Professional, to say the least. But you are nothing but a greenhorn" - He pointed a finger toward her employees – "like these kids." He eyed Akshay and Diksha and the floor, and then back to Rashmi. "They drink and puke in the office behind your back."

Rashmi glanced at Akshay and Diksha. Both bowed their heads. Rashmi now understood the reason for the stench.

Brajesh Arya stuffed his hands inside his pockets. "I made a terrible mistake by hiring you for this case. You are good enough only for the cheating spouses." He began to walk out of the office, but paused at the door. "My secretary will send you an email revoking our contract. And don't worry about the amount that I had paid you for advance. It's peanuts for me."

Money was always the top priority for Rashmi. Today, surprisingly, it wasn't.

*

Rashmi's eyes followed as Brajesh Arya and his guards left. Her eyes glued to the door even after Brajesh had left. Her mind was somewhere else.

"Boss," Akshay and Diksha said together.

Rashmi didn't respond for the first time. When they called her for the second time, she looked at them.

"Boss, we have a lot to tell you…" Diksha began, but was stopped in mid-way by Rashmi.

"I don't want to listen to anything. Brajesh Arya was right. I'm a greenhorn."

"Boss," Akshay said.

"Get out."

Akshay's heavy eyes opened wide. "We are sorry, Boss, but please listen to us for once."

"You're suspended." She pointed them toward the door. "Get out, or I will terminate you both."

Akshay opened his mouth to plead again, but Diksha nudged him with her elbow.

Slowly and sluggishly, they left the office, heads hanging low.

Rashmi didn't look at them as they left. She kept her eyes closed and fists clenched. She wasn't angry at them. She was angry at herself.

Chapter 49

Rashmi woke up at six in the morning. No matter at what time she went to sleep at night, she would invariably wake up at six.

She went for a jog for thirty minutes, and following her usual routine, she reached the grocery shop to buy milk. As she lifted the milk pouches from the blue-coloured plastic bins, the bins reminded her of the day she'd been caught and left to burn in the warehouse by Ankit Malik. It reminded her of her failure, her stupidity. *I was a bloody fool.*

She kept on staring at the bins, her mind shackled with her thoughts. She let out a heavy sigh and went ahead to the shopkeeper's desk. She paid the shopkeeper, and as always, the shopkeeper returned candies instead of the change. She didn't retaliate. She kept the candies and returned.

She realised how failure weakened a person. She was arrogant. She was cocky. This case made her a bit calmer. That was the only bright side she could think of, at least.

She returned home and slumped on the couch. She closed her eyes, despite knowing she would start remembering how she'd failed. The thoughts returned to her mind, haunting her. She recalled everything that happened in the past month—how she was tricked by Ankit Malik and Sabrina. She recalled how the evidence had been deliberately planted for her to believe in their lie, to make a fool out of her.

I am a fool. A damned, fucking fool.

She remembered the awful smile of Ankit Malik when she had been caught in the warehouse. She would have continued to brood and curse herself for her failures had the mobile phone not pinged.

It was a new WhatsApp message notification from Akshay Arora. It was a long message. Akshay had explained in the message what had exactly happened that day, followed by apologies. He seemed to be fearful of termination.

But Rashmi was barely concerned with Akshay and Diksha. Not that she was planning to kick them out; of course they were at fault, but not more than Rashmi herself. It was a completely idiotic approach to solving this case—the same old childish method of roaming around with a spy camera. This method had worked for her so far, but this wasn't a regular case, and she knew that from the start. Yet she'd followed the same method.

Brajesh Arya was right; I am nothing but a greenhorn. A cash-strapped amateur.

She opened her eyes, and her gaze fell upon the Wall of Memories. She stood up and walked up to the wall. She looked at her father, his ever-smiling, square face, his jet-black, military cut hair, his ever-suspecting, beady eyes.

Her eyes stuck on a photograph at the top-right corner. The photograph which she never wanted to be on display, but had to place on the wall on her father's requests—the photograph of her graduation. It was the time when she'd appeared for CBI exam and couldn't pass it. She felt like her entire life was a failure. She'd felt the same that day, too. And she also remembered what her father had said that day: "What's the fun in a victory which is achieved without tasting failure?"

Chapter 50

Brajesh Arya drove Rohan back from the college. His son had attended college today after quite some time today. The final semester exams were nearing and Dean had suggested him that he couldn't save Rohan from being barred from exams with zero attendance.

Brajesh Arya spent time with Rohan after college. He had to be with him because he wasn't going to be with him tonight. He'd instructed nanny that Rohan must sleep by eleven today. Rohan's phone was switched off as soon as he went to bed.

Brajesh Arya with his two personal bodyguards left home at eleven-twenty. By quarter to midnight, he reached his destination, which was in Subhash Nagar.

The stray dogs barked at his car. When he with his bodyguards hoped out with wooden baton, they fled.

The house in question was at second floor. The residents had called it a night. The lights on the first floor were off. A lone LED bulb lit up the second floor.

His bodyguards rapped the door with their knuckles.

"I think the pizza guy has arrived," a voice came from inside.

The door opened. The man inside was shirtless and wore only a brown checked boxer. His chest was sagging and so his belly. Terror swept across his chubby, acne filled face as he noticed Brajesh Arya at his doorsteps.

"What happened?" a female voice, not an Indian accent, came from one of the bedrooms.

"Who are you?" the owner of the house managed.

"Ha, you don't recognise me." Brajesh stepped inside along with his bodyguards.

One of his bodyguards shoved him and the man fell on his butt. A blonde woman, wearing only a silk dress shirt, walked out. She screamed as she noticed the intruders.

One of the bodyguards went up to him and pressed her against the wall, sealing her mouth with his thick hands.

"After the troubles you caused to me and my son," Brajesh hissed, "you don't recognise me?" He bent down, fixing Ankit Malik with his cold gaze. "Alphalion."

Chapter 51

Rashmi paid her maid extra money to clean the office. Though it was the maid's regular job to clean the office, the amount of cleaning required now, the maid declared, was over and above her regular job's requirements. Rashmi didn't mind paying her extra money, given the mess Akshay had created.

Rashmi stood at the front door, watching the maid doing the cleaning, but her mind was somewhere else. There was one question disturbing her. Why had Ankit Malik employed Karan Shukla as intern? Why was Karan Shukla so important? There was no reason to involve a college kid The only reason seemed was Rohan. Ankit Malik and Alphalion (if they aren't the same person) seemed interested in Rohan. But why? Even Karan had admitted that Ankit Malik had hired him with the condition that he would get Rohan into drugs. What would they get by getting Rohan into drugs? At the moment, only Brajesh Arya could answer this question.

But Brajesh Arya had already taken her off from the case. He was not going to entertain her any further. She didn't have the courage to call him, either. If she told him that she was still trying to solve the case, it would sound as if she was desperate to get the payment from him. This case had become more about the dignity than money.

If not Brajesh Arya, Rashmi could speak to his secretary, Pooja Sharma. Pooja was the first point of contact between her and Brajesh Arya, which meant she knew Brajesh Arya's problem. She dialled Pooja.

"Rashmi Purohit," Pooja hesitated calling her name. "How may I help you?"

"I need to know something. About Mr. Arya. About Rohan."

Pooja cleared her throat. "Mr Arya told me the case is over."

"Oh, really?" She explained the doubt she had over Rohan. "Why would Alphalion go to lengths to target Rohan? There's something wrong. And I think that was the reason Mr Arya never allowed me to meet Rohan."

"I'm just a secretary," Pooja said. "How would I know?"

"You know things which no one else in his workplace knows. The very fact that you approached me on his behalf proves my point."

Rashmi heard an exhale thrusting against Pooja's phone's mic. "It's his personal matter, Rashmi. I can't reveal his personal matters to you. It's wrong. Unethical."

"Unethical? You're talking about ethics. You hide things from the PI you hired and expect her to do miracles. How ethical is that?"

"I'm just a servant. I do what I'm asked for."

"And I hope you only want what's best for your boss and his son."

"Hmm..."

"Then tell me his problem. The truth."

Pooja remained silent for a few seconds, seemed to contemplate, weighing the options. "Someone...this Alphalion... is blackmailing Mr Arya for money."

Wow. Blackmail was the first thing she'd guessed when Brajesh Arya had contacted her for the case.

"It has to do with Rohan," Pooja said. "Alphalion has got something and using it to extort money from Mr Arya."

"And what's that thing?"

"He never told me, but last night... last night he went to... with his bodyguards he went to Ankit Malik's place."

Chapter 52

There was a time when Akshay was unemployed for months, but he wasn't unhappy. He'd left the job by himself in search of a better future. Today he was unemployed, too, but he was being fired. Suspended, his boss had called it, but it seemed he wasn't going back to the office.

He missed Pi Agency basement office. And he missed Diksha. He couldn't talk to her after that evening. While drunk, he'd told her about Smriti. He cried like a lovestruck puppy. And he'd also told her that she looked like his ex. He remembered telling her that she was beautiful. *Such an idiot you are, Akshay.* Every time he thought about that outing, a flush of embarrassment would fill his mind.

He had sent a message to boss again an hour ago, but nothing came back. He was contemplating on contacting Diksha. He wasn't sure if she would like to talk to him again. He was solely responsible for the mess.

During his last break, he would spend time in self-development. These days, he was binge watching Netflix. He was up the entire night to finish a new series, *The Witcher*. His mind searched for a new show, while his heart prodded him to ping Diksha.

He reached for his phone and opened WhatsApp. Diksha was online. He opened the chat window and wrote, "Hey. Whatsup?" His thumb hung a millimetre above the 'send' button for a heartbeat before he tapped it.

Single tick appeared. A second later another tick added. And some five six seconds later, both ticks glowed in blue.

"Hey Arora. Hw r u?" she responded.

Excitement surged through his veins seeing Diksha's message. He would feel the same when his relationship with Smriti was budding. "I'm good. And I'm sorry."

She sent a smiley and wrote, "Sorry for what?"

"For my antics that day?"

Another smiling face emoticon.

He hesitated to bring the topic of Smriti. "And those things I said about my ex, it was all just the after effects of beer. Nothing serious."

Emoticon.

"If you're free this evening," he wrote, "shall we meet over coffee? Select City Walk?"

"Don't feel like meeting anyone."

Akshay grimaced. He shouldn't have asked her out. It seemed like a desperate attempt by a heartbroken lad.

Damage control, he thought and typed, "I understand, *yaar.* We fucked up badly."

Diksha didn't respond. Neither did he make any further attempt to talk to her.

He didn't know what occur to him and he pinged Shayna Malhotra, the girl from Rohan's college whom he'd befriended and who told him about Professor Vishwas Puri. *Another desperate measure?*

"I was thinking about pinging you the other day," she wrote. *Then why didn't you?* "Oh, is it?"

"Yup. You remember I told you about that professor selling drugs to his students.

I don't want to remember it. The case has gone to the gutters. "Right."

"I've got some pics from my friends. He's sold again to a student and that student clicked his pictures in action."

He sent an astonished face emoji.

He received several images. The photographs were taken from awkward angles. The middle-aged professor with weathered face was handing over a yellow letter envelope to the receiver, whose hands were the only visible part. The photos seemed to be clicked by another student was accompanying his friend. There were photographs of the receiver pulling out a small transparent plastic bag having white powder in it.

He swiped and closely scanned all photographs. He zoomed and studied the envelopes. Yellow envelopes. He recalled Varun Mehta's testimony to boss written in boss's notepad. Varun Mehta had told him that Karan Shukla used to bring the supplies in a yellow envelope.

Is it a coincidence? *The primary tenet of sleuthing,* Rashmi

Purohit would often say, *when something has 'coincidence' written all over it, look carefully, it definitely isn't.*

"ttyl," he sent the message and closed the chat window.

The case was closed. The job was gone. Then why was he worried about who was selling drugs to whom?

A few moments of indecision passed.

He sprang from his bed. He knew what had to be done.

Chapter 53

Akshay got hold of Varun when he was about to enter into PVR Cinemas. He had managed to get Varun's phone number from Shayana, which took about an hour. But Varun was not reachable on call. Then he tried his friends and came to know that Varun was going for a movie at two in the afternoon. When he finally met Varun, he introduced himself as the colleague of the detective who'd met her a few weeks ago.

"I've told her everything I knew," Varun said. "There isn't anything to share, actually. I have not even met Rohan for a very long time."

"I need to see something," Akshay said, digging out his phone from his pocket.

Varun checked on his friends who had already passed the security check of the cinema hall. He raised his hand, gesturing them to wait. "Make it quick. The show is going to start in a while.

Akshay showed him the photographs received from Shayna, cropping out the professor purposefully. "Do you recognise this envelope?"

Varun studied the image and then looked back at him with knitted brows. "It's just another envelope."

"You told Rashmi Purohit that Karan Shukla used to bring the drugs in a yellow envelope."

Varun gave an indifferent shrug. "You can get it from any stationary shop. How can I say it's the same?"

Akshay placed his thumb and index finger on the screen and parted them without lifting the fingertips. "Look closely."

Varun's head shifted closer to the screen. A sign of recognition appeared on his face. "This" – He tapped on the screen – "this logo was there on that envelope, too, which Karan used to bring." Varun pointed single green leaf printed at the top left corner of the envelope. "Where did you get this pic from?"

Akshay couldn't help smiling. "Long story. Thanks by the way."

"Okay," Varun said, turning back, "I hope I won't be bothered again."

Can't promise. Akshay nodded. "One more question. Where I can find your friend, Adi Luthra?" Akshay wanted to corroborate this envelope logo, and the other member for Rohan's group was Adi Luthra.

"Haven't seen him in days," Varun said, spreading his both hands out, allowing the security to frisk him. "Must be out of the town for some freelancing job."

That's not good news. He now had just one source who testified that the envelopes used by Karan Shukla and Professor were same. Would it be enough for him to convince Rashmi Purohit? Would she allow him to meet at the first place?

Chapter 54

"I called you a greenhorn, Ms Purohit," Brajesh Arya said, "but I'm no less than a cunning businessman.

When Brajesh Arya contacted her last night for a meeting, she knew the exact reason. Brajesh Arya had figured out, courtesy Pi Agency, that Ankit Malik was Alphalion. He thought he wouldn't require Rashmi Purohit anymore and chucked her out of the case. That was actually a shrewd move. Akshay and Diksha's mess gave him the opportunity to expel Pi Agency out of the picture. He now knew who the Alphalion was and would take over from there. It would serve dual purpose. He wouldn't need to tell anyone about the blackmailing and he would handle Alphalion alone. Just one thing didn't fell into place – Ankit Malik wasn't Alphalion. And hence, Brajesh Arya had to come back to Rashmi.

She felt an urge to speak out her deduction, like before, but eventually chose to listen to Brajesh Arya.

"Alphalion isn't just trapping the kids into drug addictions. There is something more to it."

Rashmi frowned and leaned forward slightly.

Brajesh Arya shot a glance at the white board that still had Rohan and Alphalion's name on it. "It's really difficult for me to tell you."

Rashmi stayed quiet. She waited for Arya to reveal everything by himself.

"They are purposefully targeting the rich kids. They first get the kids of rich businessmen into addictions. Then they do something with the kid that would compromise both the kid and the parents enough to do whatever they want."

She could sense the remorse in his voice. She knew he wasn't going to hide anything from her now.

"First, they trapped my son with the help of his friends by supplying the drugs to their hostel. Once Rohan's drug use became compulsive, they stopped the supplies and started asking him to come to the places where he would get the drugs. And when he agreed to their conditions…" His eyes dropped to the floor. "They made a video of him with another man in a compromising condition."

"And they started blackmailing you. For money."

"A special kind of money. *Cryptocurrency.*"

Cryptocurrency. She had heard a lot about Bitcoin last year; a virtual currency whose price was rocketing, with new investors pouring in like wildfire.

"But he doesn't want money for himself. He wants the parents to invest the money in some specific start-ups. That's what Ankit Malik told me last night."

Rashmi was baffled.

Brajesh Arya looked away. "He doubled the amount when he came to know that I've hired you. If I can't pay, he threatened that he'll put the video on a gay porn site and will make it viral in Rohan's college."

Rashmi stared blankly at Brajesh Arya, absorbing everything he told her.

"My men roughed Ankit Malik up quite badly. Yet he didn't accept that he's Alphalion. He told us that Alphalion had helped him getting funds for his start-up. In return, he was just following his orders."

Rashmi maintained silence.

"Ms Purohit," Brajesh said, "I understand you are feeling cheated now, and I am extremely regretful. But try to understand my situation, too. I was just saving my son. It wasn't a selfish deed—my motives were never wrong."

"I understand, Mr Arya, and I am not feeling cheated. Whatever you are facing is detrimental for both your personal and professional life, in addition to the life of your son."

He released a heavy exhale of relief. His hunched shoulders now returned to relaxed state.

"I believe Ankit Malik is not lying," Rashmi said. She imagined how Ankit Malik had dropped to his knees seeing Rashmi charging at him. He didn't have the courage lie to Brajesh Arya when he'd already been mauled badly by the bodyguards. He would have spilled out everything after the first blow itself. "Now what do you want from me, Mr Arya?" she asked despite she knew the answer.

"I think we need to start from scratch now."

"We?" Rashmi smirked. "It seems you have unofficially renewed our contract."

Brajesh Arya smiled back. "I am running out of options."

Chapter 55

Rashmi stared at the Wall of Memories, her interlocked fingers resting on her lap, her eyes not blinking for once. The case was just like her current state—static. She didn't have any way out.

She looked at the different photographs of herself with her father. She got up and walked closer to them. Her shadow crawled from the floor and eclipsed the photographs. The memories, too, were nothing but shadows of her past. The memories of her past were alluring, pulling her in.

Before they could engulf her again, she moved her gaze away. It didn't help her, though. Her eyes fell on her father's bookshelf. She slowly walked up to the bookshelf and touched her father's books. Books her father always asked her to read, but she'd never read any. And there at the centre was his favourite book—*The Story of My Experiments with Truth* by Mahatma Gandhi. When Rashmi reached the age of fifteen, her father began to push her to cultivate a habit of reading, especially serious stuff.

He often encouraged her to go beyond academic books. "Textbooks will only make you a successful student," he would say. Rashmi smiled, remembering his words, "Reading is like that swinging lantern that rips through the annals of darkness. It won't show you your ultimate destination, but will light up the path toward it."

Rashmi's eyes welled up. No matter how much she tried to stay strong, the memories of her father melted her—always. She squeezed her eyes to stop the tears welling, but a trickle found its way out.

She opened her eyes. She didn't care to wipe them away. Her father's words, after all these years, had taught her something. She walked hurriedly toward the table kept in front of the couch. The pile of papers on drugs, which Akshay and Diksha had printed for her, were still lying under the table, undisturbed. She picked up an article and started reading.

The sun, after travelling all the way from east, was touching the western horizon, the tangerine light filtering in through the wide windows. Rashmi continued reading. Most of the articles she read on the drug problem pertaining to India were repetitive, and didn't offer much information. She also found some articles about how the drug cartels operated in Latin America. She took intermittent breaks when her mind would refuse to absorb any new information. There weren't many articles left, and she thought she needed to go online herself to study more. She picked up the next page, titled 'Silk Road - Bitcoin, Drugs and Dark Web'.

Silk Road, she read, was an online marketplace for buying and selling illegal drugs. The website used dark web and transactions through cryptocurrencies to hide the identity of both parties. The article piqued her interest. She never thought online buying would go to such extent. However, this site was closed in the year 2013, but it opened the door for many such illegal marketplaces expanding the listings to illegals arms and stolen credit cards.

By the time she finished the article, she dozed off on the couch.

Chapter 56

After her espresso shot, Rashmi went to the park nearby for her a jog. Monsoon was showering in all over India except for the capital. It was still hot here. A single lap and she was drowning in sweat.

"Morning, boss," she heard a voice appearing out of nowhere.

"Arora," she said, "you spooked me out."

Akshay wore an orange dry fit Nike gym t-shirt, darkened around his chest due to sweat, and black running shorts. "It had been days I did cardio," Akshay said, keeping up with her pace. "Gained a bit of fat." He pinched his belly.

"And you came all the way to this park. I'm sure you've a DDA public park in your locality.

"Just thought to see you," Akshay said, panting.

"Ahaan. You were missing me."

"I was missing Pi Agency."

She smiled. "Some important developments occurred in these days." She accelerated. Rohan took a few more seconds to keep up with her.

"Some developments at my end, too," Akshay managed through his laboured breathing.

Rashmi increased her pace, pushing herself to her limit. Akshay now lagged by a hundred meters.

She stopped when she reached failure. She stopped and bent down, resting her hands on her knees, gasping.

By the time Akshay reached, he looked like he would fall flat on his face.

"I thought you go to gym every day," she said.

Akshay took a few deep breaths before he said, "I'm more into strength training. Got work on my stamina, too."

She bolted upright, read for another lap. "Brajesh Arya came to me yesterday." She briefed Akshay about his son's true problem and his misadventure with Ankit Malik. "He wants us to resume the case."

"Are you sure he wants me back on the case?"

She chuckled. "With one condition that you won't indulge until the case is over."

"Pull your socks up, Arora," she said. Akshay's socks were literally hanging. "We don't have much time."

She darted with full speed.

"Boss," Akshay called out, "I've something to tell you."

*

"We've already messed up with a logo once," Rashmi said, looking at the photograph of Professor Vishwas Puri giving a yellow envelope to a college student.

They had come back to the office after one more lap. Akshay had requested him to switch the AC on, but she refused. "Let your sweat dry out naturally. Sudden change in temperature will make you ill."

"I think we got to give it a shot. Karan Shukla's supplier might be this professor."

"Same envelope doesn't prove anything. And moreover, Karan Shukla used to buy from KD." Fear of failure was pulling her back. She had started collecting the clues in similar fashion — a sting operation, a logo. It did nothing but screwed her up.

"May be Karan had bought from KD for once or twice."

Professor knew Rohan was a rich man's son. She'd also found during her investigation that Vishwas Puri had become rich overnight, a thing which she ignored. "You think our professor is Alphalion. And he blackmailed Brajesh Arya for money."

Akshay shrugged. "Seems a little far-fetched, but when something has written coincidence all over it..."

"It definitely isn't," Rashmi completed Akshay's sentence. *He makes sense.* And as of now she didn't have a starting point, either. She got up. "I guess need to dig out more on Vishwas Puri."

Before meeting Professor Vishwas Puri, Rashmi had to get knowledge on him more than what she had gathered last time. She was interested in his financial condition this time. She remembered from her previous visit the bank and credit card statements kept under his coffee table. She'd to sift through her contacts for a friend in a bank.

She found a friend from college time, Manoj Kalra, who was in the same bank. The same guy who'd told her, "Dusky is the new sexy." She'd stumbled across him in a shopping mall a year ago when he was shopping with his fiancée. They'd exchanged the numbers, out of formality.

"Hello, dusky is the new sexy," Manoj greeted her.

She gave a soft chuckle. "You still remember that?"

"I even remembered it the day we met last year. Couldn't say though. My fiancée was with me. I would've been divorced before the marriage." He let out a hearty laugh.

"I need a favour." It didn't feel right contacting him after this long, only for a work which was illegal. But she needed inside information on Vishwas Puri's financials to tackle him. "There is a guy who's got an account in your bank."

"New case," Manoj said in a playful tone.

"This guy turned rich overnight. Would like to know how his fortune turned."

Manoj Kalra agreed to help without a hint of hesitation. And that made her feel guilty even more. She had cut herself off from family and friends, thinking that they would never be required. They had never existed for her until now. But when the need came, they treated her as if she was always with them.

Chapter 57

Rashmi's last conversation with Vishwash Puri was superficial. That time she had only vague information from a college student. This time she had evidence. *Let's see where the logo takes us this time.*

Vishwas Puri squinted as he saw Rashmi at his doorsteps. "Ms Detective?"

"Rashmi Purohit."

"How may I help you?" He didn't welcome her this time. The door was opened as much as a gash on the skin.

"I've some questions for you?"

"Drugs again?"

She nodded.

He opened the door with great effort as if he was opening the gigantic doors of a palace. He didn't ask her to have a seat.

"Let me come straight to the point," she fished out her phone from her pocket. "Where do you buy the drugs from?"

Anger flashed across professor's scruffy face. "Is it an allegation?"

"It is an enquiry, sir."

He finally offered her a seat, and sank into the couch with a scowl. "Tell me what you want?"

She tilted her head. "You know my question."

"How can you assume I sell drugs to college students?"

She threw a deliberate grin at him. "I never said that you sell drugs to college students."

Vishwas Puri exhaled, looking on the floor.

"You're a compulsive gambler. You lost quite a good some of money in stock market," she began to gloat the information she'd obtained from her friend, "the reason for your wife's departure. But it didn't stop you. You invested in cryptocurrencies as well. No luck. And then a brilliant idea sparked in the crooked head of yours. Trapping the rich kids into drug addiction, shoot compromising videos, and blackmail their parents for money in the form of cryptocurrencies. And boom" – she looked around his house – "you are suddenly rich."

His face remained calm for a long time and then he smiled. "You could be a good fiction writer. I like your story, but unfortunately, you have zero evidence."

She crossed her hands and leaned back. "Sir, I know people in the top brass. The who's who of the capital. After I'm done here, I've dinner planned with an old friend who happens to be in Delhi Police." She knew she'd gone overboard, but a little exaggeration could give an edge to her threats. "Plus, I've photographs of your last drug transaction," she added.

The professor let out a loud hum. He got up and tottered to the wooden TV cabinet and pulled the drawer out. "It seems you've gone to lengths to dig things about me."

"A kid's life is at stake."

The professor kept on rummaging the drawer. It felt odd. Rashmi got to her feet and stepped toward.

Professor Puri swivelled, swinging his hand, in his hand were a pair of scissors. Rashmi pulled her head back. The scissor whizzed past, barely escaping her nose.

"You think you walk into my place and can threaten me?" He charged at her with swinging scissor like a sword. It seemed his back problem had suddenly disappeared. The features of his bedraggled face changed rapidly. "You think you can stop me. Even my wife couldn't stop me." His gritting teeth gave him a look of wolf, and he charged at her like one.

Rashmi staggered back and hit the couch on which she was sitting. She lost balance dropped on the couch. The professor approached her even before she could regain her balance. She got hold of the cushion kept on the couch and used it as a shield against the scissor. The cushion was not strong enough to save her from scissor, but the scissor was no sword, too.

She managed to stop the scissor before Vishwas Puri could stab her. The cushion cover gave up and the scissor tore apart the fabric, finding its place among the cotton fillings.

The professor pulled back the scissor and attacked a bit higher, on her head. Rashmi grabbed his hand, stopping his weapon inches above her forehead. Even at this age, professor had a good strength. The scissor was evenly poised between two opposing forces.

Rashmi yelled, twisting professor's hands with all the strength she had got. A couple of bones cracked and professor wailed in agony.

She pushed herself onto her feet, professor's hand still in her grasp. Professor Puri's eyes welled with the tears of pain. She kicked on his back and he thudded on the sleek marble floor. "Fun's over," she said, huffing air out of his lungs.

Chapter 58

Professor Vishwas Puri lay sprawled on the couch, his good hand clasping the broken one, his legs spread out making a V.

"What were you trying to do professor?" Rashmi asked, her hands crossed, boring her steady glare on him. "What would you have done even if you'd managed to hurt me… or kill me?"

He groaned, flinching with pain. "It was an impulsive act. I'm no blackmailer, Ms –"

"Rashmi Purohit," she said.

"Yeah, Yeah," he said, "Rashmi Purohit. I keep on forgetting your name." He fidgeted on the couch. "I lost money in stocks and cryptocurrencies. Yes, I sold drugs to my students as well to keep cover for my soaring debts and credit card bills. It's the Cricket betting that made me rich. Premier League's last season turned out to be extremely lucky to me. Trust me. I didn't blackmail any student. I could never do that."

"Trust. Saying a teacher who is pushing his students into the cycle of addiction."

He winced. "I know I did bad things. Really nasty things. But I took money from dangerous people. I was in Queer street. The act was out of desperation."

"The reason behind every crime is desperation, sir. Yours is no different."

His face contorted with pain and guilt. "I'm sorry. That's all I can say."

"Sorry won't work, sir. I need answers from you."

His finally found courage to meet eyes with her, his mouth slightly opened.

"The yellow envelope you used to pack drugs. What's that?"

He stared into the false ceiling, as if rummaging his memory for the details of the envelope. "It was… it was a packaging, I received the delivery in the same packaging."

"Delivery? Who sold you?

Professor Puri gulped. His mouth opened and then closed and then opened again. "I bought it online?"

"Online?" Rashmi squeaked.

"I know it sounds weird, but there's a website from which you can buy all illegal drugs, delivered to your doorsteps."

"Like those e-commerce websites? Like Amazon."

"Exactly. Like Amazon."

The article she read the other day flashed in her mind. She put effort on her memory to recall the name. Silk Road it was. An American online store for buying illegal drugs. Silk Road had been developed and run by a twenty-five-year-old USA-based physicist, Ross Ulbricht. Ross had run the website on an anonymous browser, Tor, and employed cryptocurrencies as the mode of payment. Silk Road, however, had been busted in 2013.

"A student had told me about it," Vishwas Puri said, "I don't remember his name.

Karan Shukla, Rashmi thought.

"But I found it the best way to get drugs," Vishwas Puri added. "There was no risk of going to the dark alleys and shady corners of the city, meeting with unknown, potentially criminal people, to buy drugs. I can buy with a mere click of a mouse."

Karan Shukla would've been a frequent buyer from this website. Varun Mehta confirmed that to Arora. His drug trade and Rohan's entrapment was connected. So Alphalion could very well be connected to this online drugs website. "Show me how you buy from it."

"I... I don't remem..."

Rashmi spoke before he could finish his prolonged 'remember', "You want me to break that other arm, too?"

"No, please. If you bring my laptop from the room, I can show you. As you see..." He pointed with his chin toward his right hand.

Rashmi went to his study and grabbed his laptop. She opened the lid and powered it on. She kept in on professor's lap sat beside it.

Professor used his left hand to open the special browser called Tor. He typed one letter after another with his left hand, slowly and painfully.

Rashmi was by now stripped of patience. She took hold of the laptop. "I don't have a lifetime for this. Let me do it."

Professor dictated the entire hyperlink.

The home page appeared on the screen. At the top right corner was a green leaf logo, the one from the yellow envelope. She spotted the name of the website below the logo – IndiParadise.

Vishwas Puri took her to a tour of the website. Every single illegal drug could be found there. It was really a paradise for the addicts.

"I already had invested in cryptocurrencies. So I thought why not use them to buy drugs and sell them for hard cash. I ordered a small quantity for the first time, and I didn't have much hope that it would actually come to my doorsteps. But it really did, just like any other product bought online. Slowly it became normal. And then an addiction."

Rashmi shook her head. "I've one last question for you. I asked you this question when we last met and you gave an Oscar winning performance to dodge this question. But this time I need the truth."

Vishwas Puri waited for the answer wearing a look of anticipation on his crinkled face.

"Who's Alphalion?"

Vishwas Puri took the laptop back from his left hand. It almost fell from his hand. He made a few clicks and showed the screen to her. "I don't know his true identity, but he's the one who runs this website.

Chapter 59

The lights, as always, were off. It was dark. *Dark web. Alphalion is hiding somewhere in the darkness. Dark web. Watching my every move. He'd always been one step ahead of me. Several steps, actually.*

Professor Vishwas Puri had pleaded her not to reveal this side of her to anyone. "I'm not going to do that," she'd said. "Your students will decide your fate." She left the decision with the students whether they would want to expose Vishwas Puri or not.

Rashmi dug out more articles on Silk Road from the internet. After Silk Road's closure, a lot of copy-cats had sprung up throughout the world, and had soon been busted up as well. Now with professor's revelation, she speculated that perhaps someone had used the same method and opened an India-based online drug store, a kind of Indian Silk Road. With the boom in e-commerce in India, and almost all service fields going online, it would not be surprising if someone had come up with the idea of an online drug store.

Indiparadise. I've been hunting Alphalion down nearly everywhere. These shabby ghettos. These glassy corporate buildings. But all along he was he was hiding in the filth of dark web.

Online drug selling seemed to be compatible with an additional service of arranging funds for start-ups by trapping the children of rich people and blackmailing them. The owner of the site would then have some share of the start-up's earnings. That was how Alphalion made Ankit Malik to do things as per his whims and fancies. The more the start-ups he would fund, the more his earnings would be. Moreover, Brajesh Arya had been asked to invest via cryptocurrencies, again compatible with how the online store worked.

Her phone lit up, killing the darkness. The silence too was killed by the ringtone. She eyed the display – Brajesh Arya.

"Ms. Purohit," Brajesh Arya's voice trembled as if it he was standing inside an igloo. "Did you hear the news?"

"About what?" Rashmi asked.

"It's all over the local news. Ankit Malik has disappeared."

Rashmi tucked her phone under her head and shoulder and typed on Google, "Ankit Malik Pigeon Delivery."

The result displayed: "Owner of Logistics Start-Up Pigeon Delivery Mysteriously Disappears." There were a number of such headlines.

"I think Alphalion figured out that I had been interrogating him." His every word was laced with fear.

"And they've now removed the weak link," Rashmi said. A thought came to her mind, and she said, "Mr. Arya, I will call you back."

She cut the line and called Adi Luthra. He didn't pick the call. She then dialled Varun Mehta.

Varun picked up in two rings.

"Did you meet Karan recently?" she asked.

"How… what… how do you," Varun Mehta couldn't complete his sentence.

"What?"

"He's dead, ma'am. He is run over by a truck this evening…"

Chapter 60

It was five minutes to five PM and it was burning outside like a blast furnace. July was over, but monsoon was nowhere to be seen.

Earlier today, boss had asked him to contact Diksha and ask her to resume her job. Diksha said she was sick and wouldn't join anytime sooner. It seemed odd. Akshay left office early today so that he would find the gym thinly populated, but on his way back, he decided to drop by Diksha. He'd never gone to her place, but it had been days he'd seen her. *You really want to see her, man? Really want to remember Smriti again?*

His heart got the better of his brain and he reached outside her PG. He called her.

"Why are you here?" she sounded annoyed.

"You said you're not well. Boss asked me to drop by."

She cut the call. Akshay wasn't sure what did that mean. He chose to stay for a while.

The door to her house opened and she came out. She wore a gray wrinkled T-shirt having written I 'heart' NY and black shorts with tiny red hearts dotted all across. Her hair was not as straight as it would normally be, and bangs covered half of her face. She did look sick, though.

Akshay put his scooter on side stand and approached her. "Hey, how have you been?"

She glared at him, her lips pressed together. "Why are you here?"

"Our suspension has ended. Brajesh Arya has hired us back."

"Good," she said and looked away.

"When are you coming back?"

"Has she really sent you to ask about me?"

Akshay took a beat before responding. "Yes."

She scoffed. "Really? Does she think of anything else other than her company and her case?"

Akshay sighed. "She's got attitude problem."

"She's got a lot of problems," Diksha snapped. "All mental problems. You know what she did that day. We were almost killed. And what she did. Fired us."

"She was almost killed, too."

Diksha crossed her hands, staring into the air. "I've barely finished the year one of my work-life and I have been fired twice."

"You're not fired, Diksha. We were not fired. Just a temporary suspension."

She gave a sardonic smile.

"We need you, Diksha. Pi Agency needs you."

"She doesn't need me. She never includes me in any detective work. And for you, you don't need me. You just need to see this" – She circled the air in front of her face – "this face, which looks like your ex."

It felt like a punch burrowed in his gut. Diksha showed him the truth quite brutally. "It's… it's not true. Half of the things I said that day were just booze-tipped talks."

"I don't know about you, Arora, but I'm not here for these stupid things. My entire life is at stake. I ran from Gujarat for a job. If I go back, my father would tie me up with the son of some diamond merchant or an industrialist. I don't have time for this petty romance. I need a job. Bet it a ten thousand per month job or five thousand."

"Then come back to the job you had. The job you still have."

She sighed. "You won't get it, Arora." She turned back and left.

He saw it right then. It was evident, right there, in her eyes. She wasn't the same Diksha anymore. The one he'd always known. The devil-may-care girl, ever-so-cheerful, the one so full of intoxications of life.

He couldn't fathom what had broken inside her. Was it the conversation they had or was it Rashmi Purohit's treatment a week ago?

Whatever it was, he felt a part of him too suffered from collateral damage. He watched her walk off, the bounce missing in her gait, disappearing inside the house without a second glance backward toward him.

Chapter 61

When Rashmi rang the doorbell of this house in the locality of Subhash Nagar, she was sure who would appear behind the door. Although, she didn't expect her face would appear completely different to what she was accustomed to see.

"Rashmi," Sabrina said. She hesitated before letting Rashmi in.

Her rumpled hair was tied clumsily into a ponytail. Her eyes emerald pupil now looked dull as algae. A darker shade of her ivory-complexion rimmed her eyes.

As Rashmi stepped in, a strong malodour of cigarette filled her nostrils. Wreaths of smoke hovered over the living room like mountain mist. A moment later she spotted buds of the source of smell scattered on the floor. Two bottles of wine were disposed on the floor.

The way Sabrina hobbled across the room and slouched on the bean bag, Rashmi figured out she was drunk.

"My neck still hurts, Sab," Rashmi said.

Sabrina smiled wryly. "The day they were tying you on the chair, leaving alone to be burnt alive, I knew that wasn't your fate." She reached for one the wine bottles and swallowed the last drops left inside it. "You never give up. I saw it in your eyes. I knew you would bounce back, and appear at my doorsteps." She paused. "Ankit Malik's doorsteps – because it's his house – one day."

"And still you chose Ankit Malik's side."

"All this," Sabrina rasped, "not a speck of dust here is mine. And you expect me to go against Ankit."

"And now he's gone."

Misery overtook Sabrina's composure. She put her hand on her mouth and broke into tears. "He killed Ankit. Alphalion killed him."

Rashmi exhaled. "There's no corpse yet to certify that. He could still be out there, hiding."

Rashmi made no attempt to console her. It took Sabrina over a minute to regain her composure. She plucked out a Marlboro from the pack and lit it up. Rashmi shortened her breathing. The white smoke began to choke her.

"Sorry." Sabarina dabbed the cigarette on the floor as she noticed Rashmi waving the smoke off with her hand.

"I'm not here to offer you sympathy," Rashmi said. "I'm up against Alphalion. Ankit Malik was the only person who was affiliated with Alphalion, and you are the only person who was close to Ankit Malik. I want your help."

"I don't know who Alphalion is. I'm not sure even Ankit knew about him."

Rashmi explained her about Indiparadise and its creator – Alphalion. "Think from this perspective now. Rack your brains. May be you'll find something that can help us unmask this hidden enemy. I'm sure you want justice."

"I don't want justice." Rage accentuated Sabrina's heavy breathing. "I want this Indiparadise burnt to ashes."

Chapter 62

Brajesh Arya was the first one to join the meeting which Rashmi had set up today. He came even before her employees. *Perhaps he should give a lesson or two on punctuality to the kids*, she thought.

"Good morning, Ms Purohit," Brajesh Arya said. He scanned the room. "You have converted this basement into an office pretty smartly."

"Necessity is the mother of invention," Rashmi said.

"Right," he said as he looked around, as if searching for something. He observed the AC and looked down at the remote control which was slotted into the remote holder mounted on the wall. "20 degrees," he murmured. He was in the same crisp formal suit, but of a different shade.

How can he deal with a suit in this blistering summer? Rashmi thought.

Purushottam Purohit was the next one to join. She had requested her uncle join the meeting, as she believed his experience might help her. Arora was the next to join. Diksha hadn't resumed office since the day she sent both her employees to a forced sabbatical.

"Indiparadise," Brajesh Arya read out the words displayed on the projector screen, which was actually a white board. "The ultimate gateway to the paradise."

Once she'd learned about Indiparadise, she downloaded Tor on her laptop and accessed the website. As the webpage opened, a white screen appeared with the green leaf icon. Below the icon was 'Indiparadise' in bold font, with the tagline: 'the ultimate gateway to paradise'.

"So you think this is the website through which Rohan and his friends used to buy the drugs?" Brajesh Arya asked.

"Karan, to be precise," Rashmi corrected him. "Karan was the one who used to buy drugs online, as per Rohan's other two friends." Rashmi narrated the events that led her to Indiparadise.

"Morning, everyone." Diksha entered the office, clutching her laptop bag in front of her stomach. Her face was dull and eyes were down. Nothing about her seemed okay, probably because she was sick.

"Hi," Akshay whispered, waving her hand.

Diksha walked across the office and sat beside Arora.

"And you know who runs this website? Alphalion." She pointed at the username of the creator of Indiparadise."

Barjesh Arya and her uncle nodded, while Akshay and Diksha appeared to be still grasping what Rashmi had explained.

"So, we have the bull's eye now," her uncle said, "and believe me, it's the easiest target you could possibly imagine." Her uncle walked near the screen. "Our enemy," he said, pointing his finger at the Indiparadise logo, "is essentially hidden behind this website. If we can hack into this website, or know the IP address from which this website is running, we can find who is running it. We will pretty much get the person in question."

Akshay cleared his throat and said, "Then, sir, this is the most difficult target we could possibly have."

Purushottam smirked, discounting the kid's opinion. "And why so?"

"Because he is hidden behind Tor," Akshay declared. "*The Tor.*"

"What's so special about this Tor?" Purushottam asked as he returned to his seat.

Akshay straightened his back and turned toward others. "Normally, when we access a website, the transaction of the data happens between the user and the website. Both of us have a clear view of each other's IP addresses. But when both use Tor, both parties cannot know each other's IP addresses. Tor is specially designed for this very purpose—hiding the IP address, maintaining anonymity."

Rashmi had heard about Tor's power of anonymity when she had read about Silk Road. But she didn't care to go deep into the nuts and bolts of this technology. "But there should be some way to break into Tor and find the real IP," she said.

"Unfortunately, no," Akshay said.

"Maybe Mr. Arya can help us in finding some advanced hackers who could do that?" She turned to Brajesh Arya.

"No hacker could unmask the person behind Tor just like

that," Akshay insisted, appearing to be losing his cool. Rashmi's comment seemed to have struck his ego. "Because Tor transmits the information through multiple nodes, or IPs, the data emerging from the source travels through multiple IPs before it reaches the destination. So no one could know the actual IP of the destination if he is monitoring the destination, or the actual IP of the source, if he is monitoring the source."

Everyone stared at Akshay again.

"Okay," Akshay said, "let me explain it to you in simple words. Suppose I have to send a card to Mr. Arya. Normally, I would write Mr. Arya's address and my address on the card. If anyone monitors my shipment, he could easily identify the two parties. Now, if I write only Mr. Arya's address on the card and put it inside an envelope with Purushottam uncle's address on it. Then I enclose it inside a second envelope with Boss's address on it. And finally, I put it inside a third envelope with Diksha's address on it. Now I send this packet to Diksha first. Diksha will open that envelope and send it to our boss. Boss, in turn, will open it and send it to Uncle Purushottam, and lastly, Purushottam uncle will send it to Mr. Arya. Only at the first transaction is my address revealed, and only at the last transaction is Mr. Arya's address is revealed.

"This means no one can relate me to Mr Arya or otherwise. Now you get how Tor works? Everyone peels a layer, like an onion, and transfers the data to other. That's what Tor means— T.O.R, The Onion Router."

"And what if someone in between opens all envelopes at once and sees the destination's address?" Purushottam asked.

Akshay smiled, as if he was waiting for the question to come. "Every transaction is encrypted with a key. This means you have the key to open only the envelope you have received, not other envelopes."

There was an intermission of grim silence in the basement. Rashmi, after absorbing Akshay's explanation, spoke, "So, there is absolutely no way to find the identity of Indiparadise owner?"

Akshay sighed heavily. "There is a way called a correlation attack, which the authorities use to break through that anonymity. Needless to say, it requires a lot of time and effort, and most importantly, resources that we don't have."

"So we are stuck at a dead end," Rashmi said, looking away from everyone. Again. "Akshay and Diksha," she called out her subordinates loudly, "I want both of you to get deeper into this website. Get into each and every corner of this website. There must be something which will lead us to the core of Indiparadise."

Not everyone in life got second chance. Her Papa never got one. She'd got several chances for CBI, she failed at every chance. Now Brajesh Arya had given Pi Agency a second chance. She had no other option.

I'm not going to fail again, Papa.

Chapter 63

Akshay was frightened for the first time in this case. He was supposed to be scared when the unknown attackers had attacked him, but thankfully, alcohol had made him immune to fear that time. But today, he knew they were definitely not going to succeed in this case; their enemy was hidden behind Tor. Even the USA's FBI couldn't break through the security of Tor so easily. He didn't stand a chance. He'd explained everything to his boss, yet she was hopeful that they would get something to yield the identity of the Tor, which would compromise their high-end technology!

Only thing that brought him delight today was Diksha's return. When she'd entered the office this morning, he felt like running up to her and pulling her into an embrace. But that would be weird. To the two gentlemen, to boss, and to himself, too.

The meeting had ended, and the two gentlemen were about to leave.

"I'm sorry, Mr Arya," Akshay said, "for all those stupid things I did that day."

"Rookie error," Brajesh Arya said. "Everyone does that in the beginning. Even I've done many." He then pointed at the floor. "Except for that."

And everyone broke into a friendly laughter.

Akshay, with his boss and Diksha, came out to see off Brajesh Arya and Purushottam Purohit. His boss, along with Diksha, was busy in talking with Brajesh Arya, while his uncle was ambling toward his car.

Purushottam stopped and said with raised brows, "You are...."

"Akshay," Akshay said.

"Yes, Akshay, come with me."

Akshay followed him.

As Purushottam reached near his car, he said, "How long have you been with Rashmi?"

"Two years," Akshay answered. "Almost from the conception of Pi Angecy."

"Good. So you and that girl, Diksha, are the only human beings with whom she is spending most of her time."

Akshay chuckled and nodded.

Purushottam clambered inside the car making deep groan. "Your boss seems quite tough. The no-nonsense detective, right?"

Akshay shrugged.

"But the truth is…she's not. She is broken inside. She is alone, very alone in her life. And she loves it. God knows why she loves this loneliness. But she needs to be taken out of this loneliness…" He paused for a moment. "Rescued from this loneliness. She will never tell you anything, never express anything, but she needs to be saved from it."

Akshay was finding it difficult to understand what boss's uncle was trying to convey.

Purushottam continued, "I just…I just want to say…to take care of her….please. Be with her, always."

Purushottam drove the car away, and so did Brajesh Arya. Akshay turned to see her boss; there was only Diksha, lost in her thoughts.

Boss had returned to the office…alone.

Chapter 64

Rashmi had come home during the semester break vacation. The penultimate semester of her graduation had finished, and only six months of study in her degree remained. After dinner, she was checking her college website for the companies that were going to visit next semester for campus placement. Her parents were talking to each other in the dining room, but she wasn't paying much attention.

Her father's voice, a loud one, came suddenly. "Madhu, have you gone mad?"

"Dheeraj don't raise your voice," Madhu, Rashmi's mother, said.

"You are mother of a twenty-three-year-old girl. How could you think of—"`

"Dheeraj, please. She can hear us."

Rashmi stood up and quietly walked up to the edge of the door. She couldn't see them from here, and they couldn't see her, either, but she could now listen to them clearly.

Dheeraj lowered his voice. "What is your problem? Tell me. A divorce is not a solution."

A ripple of fear spread through Rashmi's chest at hearing the word 'divorce'.

"I've spent my entire life looking after you and your daughter. I killed my dreams. Now I want to live out my dreams."

"Your daughter? She's our daughter, Madhu. And I have never stopped you from chasing your dreams. You are free to do whatever you want to do."

"My dreams were killed the day I had been married to you." There was bitterness in Madhu's voice, for Dheeraj, for their married life. "What do Indian parents expect of a girl? Taking care of her husband and his family, and then taking care of her child. How was I supposed to pursue my dreams? How was I supposed to think of my career?"

"Madhu," Dheeraj said after a long pause, "you can still do whatever you want. No one is going to stop you. I will help you with whatever you want to do. We will do it together." Dheeraj was almost pleading.

"Together!" Madhu smirked. "I don't want to explain anything else. It is going to hurt you."

"Tell me. I am ready to listen to you. Anything to save our marriage."

"I never wanted to marry you. I never wanted to marry anyone. I wanted to start a work of my own. Build a business of my own. But I had been tied to you. I could have left you after our marriage, but I respect my parents, and yours, too. I understand our social standing. And then Rashmi was born. I couldn't think leaving you and a child alone. I took care of her, right from childhood till this very day. I never told you that I wanted to do anything other than taking care of our family. But now Rashmi is going to finish her studies and will get a job soon. It's the right time for me to drift away from this life."

"You don't need to drift away from me," Dheeraj said. "We will both work together. We will start something new, whatever you would like to."

"I don't need your help," Madhu said. "You are a government employee. You have had job security right from the first day of your work. How can you help with a business?"

Dheeraj didn't say anything. His silence demonstrated his pain.

"I have already thought of everything," Madhu said. The chair squealed. "I have got a partner as well. I am just waiting to start."

Rashmi heard footsteps approaching toward kitchen, which was beside her room. She quickly got back to her computer so that her mother wouldn't find her listening to her parents' conversation. Her parents didn't speak after that. Nor did they speak in the morning. Rashmi didn't have the courage to ask anything about it, either.

After six months, after she took her last exam, her father told her that her mother had left them. It had been more than a month since she'd left, but he hadn't told her at the time, as he didn't want to put her through mental stress during her exams.

It wasn't that Rashmi wasn't prepared for it, but she'd hoped her father would sort things out. She hoped her mother wouldn't be so selfish as to leave her husband and her daughter to pursue her own wishes. But she had to accept the truth. She couldn't, after all, stop her mother from doing what she had decided to do. No one could have.

Rashmi returned home after she'd finished college. She didn't express anything to her father—neither grief nor anguish. She was never expressive; neither was her father. They both understood that they'd moved on.

Except for the fact the she didn't. Her hatred for her mother kept growing by the day. Her father never complained about his wife, but he gradually became a recluse. His hair started greying quickly. The only wish in his life was to see his daughter become a CBI officer. And his daughter had failed him—just like his wife.

Rashmi joined a private security firm. Time lapsed, but she didn't see any happiness in her father's face. That was a constant reminder for her that she had failed him.

She'd then started Pi Agency. Her father resisted, but didn't push her much. It seemed that he was not interested in living anymore. He was just waiting for death. And it was true. He died a few months after Rashmi had started Pi Agency.

She was left with nothing and no one in her life, except for Pi Agency. She immersed herself completely in her work to escape from the emotions and feelings; the pain of her father's death, the rage of her mother's departure from her life.

But one day, unexpectedly, shortly after her father's demise, her mother visited her office. Her mother was a software engineer and had partnered with a college mate to start an internet forum. The user base grew reasonably in those years, and by now, the website was doing pretty well.

Madhu had called Rashmi to pay her condolences for Dheeraj's demise. She didn't speak as though it was her husband who had died. The actual reason, though, behind Madhu's call was to meet Rashmi. Rashmi blatantly refused to meet her. But their meeting was not a proposal from Madhu—it was a declaration.

Rashmi was busy writing a report for a client when Madhu entered the office. She looked around the basement office and gave a contemptuous smile. "I'm sorry for your loss, beta. How are you?"

"Why are you here?" Rashmi snapped.

Madhu took a seat. She was wearing smart formal attire. Her naturally curly hair was now straightened. She looked much younger than she actually was. "I know you are angry at me, rather mad. And it is justified, too. But imagine what would have happened if your father had married you to someone else when you were thinking of opening this agency?"

Rashmi stayed quiet, glowering at her mother.

Madhu put her elbows on the table and leaned confidently toward Rashmi. She was wearing a silver Fossil watch. Her wedding ring was absent. "I bet you would have refused to marry someone at all. But we weren't so daring those days. We weren't asked for approval before we were married to anyone. I had to blindly accept what my father had told me to do."

Rashmi gaze grew intense. "So you are here to justify what you did to my father?"

"No, I am not," Madhu straightened. "I don't have to. What I did was right, and what is right doesn't need justification."

"You think it was right," Rashmi whetted her tone. "I think it was wrong as hell. As selfish as it can get. Let's agree to disagree. You are free to leave."

Madhu opened her mouth, and Rashmi was ready to reciprocate, to let off steam, to give vent to the rage she had kept inside her heart for her mother all these years. But Madhu stopped herself. Her tough expression melted down.

"I came here for you," Madhu said. "I knew how alone you would be feeling right now. That's why I came here. After all, I am your mother. I am here to take you with me."

Rashmi found it more amusing than surprising. She hadn't spoken to her once after she'd abandoned her husband and her daughter. And now she has come to show her care. She let her mother continue to speak.

"How long can you earn your bread and butter from this agency, Pi Agency, or whatever you call it? You are a brilliant girl, and this private investigation thing doesn't suit you. Come with me and join my organisation. You will get a good position and good compensation."

It was Rashmi who gave a contemptuous smile this time. "Is it a job interview? Let me be very clear, ma'am. I would rather die penniless than work in that organisation which was built by compromising my father's happiness."

Madhu huffed. "So, you want to spend rest of your life in this stuffy basement which you call an office? I am a self-made businesswoman, and I know what it takes to run a business. You're doomed, girl. You won't even be able to run this company for a year. And when all doors are closed, you will come to me, begging—mark my words, begging."

Madhu stood up, pushing the chair back, and stomped out of the office.

Pi Agency was now more than two years old. Rashmi had been working day and night to show her mother what Pi Agency was capable of. She had come a long way since then. Her company was still a small fry—even smaller than some of the start-ups. But she had never failed any of her clients, and she was striving to achieve the same for Brajesh Arya, too. It was the biggest case Pi Agency had ever dealt with, and if she could pull off this case, it was going to be the biggest achievement in Pi Agency's history. It would make her future happen.

Chapter 65

Akshay's eyes had been fixed on the Indiparadise logo for the past twenty minutes. He was still learning the art of hacking a website, and now, his boss had given a daunting task of hacking a website equipped with the anonymiser, Tor. He started with looking at the products listed on the website. He could identify the known drugs like cocaine, heroin, LSD, and weed. But there were some unknown pharmaceutical drugs like phensedyl and spasmoproxyvyon as well.

He'd never been a drug guy. He wasn't even a liquor guy. He couldn't get himself to have anything stronger than beer. His friends often mocked him for not been able to have 'hard drinks' like whisky, but he was happy with limiting himself to beer. During his engineering days, he had been offered by his friends—rather, forced—to join those weed sessions, but he would always run away from the hostel and hide inside the library for the whole night.

And he rightly did so. One of his friends had suffered nervous breakdown from opium abuse. His parents had to leave their jobs and shift to the city where their college was based. They had to stay with their son and take care of him for one year. It was painful to see his parents paying for their son's deed. He had decided since that day that he would not, for his own pleasure, ever stoop to such a situation.

He kept on wandering through the website, noticing the variety of products listed, from small to large quantities. Each product had a number of sellers offering different prices, making it easier for buyers to get the best deal. Across the table his boss, too, was engrossed with the drug portal. Diksha had left, but boss and he had been continuing. It was nine, and they had already stretched three hours past their official closing hour. No one was getting anywhere.

"People generally tend to keep the same usernames across different social media platforms," Rashmi suggested. "Why not check people with username Alphalion on all social media platforms?"

"No luck, boss." He'd looked people with the same username on Twitter, Facebook, and Instagram. The results showed hundreds of people. It was nothing less than finding a needle in a haystack.

"How about extracting the email ID of Alphalion from Indiparadise website?" Rashmi asked. "There might be an option to send an email to the admin."

Akshay had already thought about it. "Tor has an option of Tor chat. So the admin speaks to the customers and sellers via Tor chat."

Rashmi winced. "Fuck," she muttered.

"Frisking this website as a buyer won't help, boss" Akshay said, leaning back, clasping his hands behind his head. "We got to infiltrate as a seller."

"For creating a seller account, you need to upload your government photo ID." It seemed Rashmi had already done the research. "I'm not going to allow any of us to give our IDs to a criminal website."

"Our options are already very limited."

Rashmi closed shut the laptop down. "We'll find some way." She stood and stretched herself. "If you want, you can stay back at my place today."

Boss had offered her to stay at her house that night as well when they had come back from their ordeal at KD's home. He only had a professional relation with boss. She never asked anything about his personal life ever. So going to her personal space, and sleeping there, was a little awkward.

"She is broken inside," Prushottam uncle's words rang in his ears. *"She is alone, very alone in her life. And she loves it… She will never tell you anything, never express anything, but she needs to be saved from it."*

"Okay." He sighed. "I'll stay back."

Chapter 66

Rashmi opened the door of her house and switched the lights on. Akshay waited for her to ask him to enter her house.

"Come," she said.

As Akshay entered, his eyes wandered across the living room. His gaze then rested upon the wall right at the front of the door, a wall with some eight to ten photographs.

"I am sorry, Arora," Rashmi said, "you need to make yourself comfortable on the couch. The second bedroom is stuffed with old things."

"Not an issue," Akshay said, observing closely the photographs.

"This is my father's house," Rashmi said, "in the truest sense. I haven't added a single item to this house since I inherited it from him."

It seemed a daunting task to live in this house alone. Akshay reasoned that boss was probably living here because it reminded her of her father. Rashmi bade him goodnight and closed the door of her room.

He sank on the couch. Thankfully, there was a window AC in the living room. He studied the wall of photographs. In the majority of the photographs, Rashmi was with her father, and in some, she was alone. *Why none with her mother?*

He passed some time by watching a couple of episodes of Locke & Key. His phone's battery gave up when he was barely five minutes into the third. He connected his phone to the charging point, which was a few feet away from the couch. He came back to the couch and stared blankly at the ceiling. His sight fell on the bookshelf. He walked up to the shelf and scanned the books.

The Story of My Experiments with Truth. The book caught his attention, and he drew it out of the shelf. As he flipped through the pages, an envelope dropped on the floor. He bent down and picked it up. The envelope was sealed. *Boss never opened it?*

He was going to put it back, but the temptation to open a

sealed envelope didn't let him set it aside. He looked all around the envelope. Blank. The paper had paled.

He glanced toward the bedroom—the door had been shut. He returned to the couch with the envelope. He thought for a while and tore the envelope carefully along the seal. There was an A4 sheet inside, folded thrice. He unfolded the sheet.

The letters were handwritten by blue ink. It started with Beta and ended with Papa.

It took him only a minute or so to finish reading it, but when he was done, his eyes had moistened.

Chapter 67

"I told you we aren't doing this." Rashmi was fuming. She had told Akshay specifically last night that they wouldn't create a seller account on Indiparadise. And the first thing in the morning Akshay did was create a seller account by the name of *Striker1*.

"It's okay, boss," Akshay said. "We knew the risks before we took up this case."

"No, it's not okay." A pang of guilt stung her heart. "She was putting this kid on the line of fire."

"Know your enemies," Akshay said, a smile appearing at the corner of his mouth. "You remember that?"

If you know your enemies and know yourself, you will not be imperiled in a hundred battles. If you do not know your enemies, nor yourself, you will be imperilled in every single battle, Rashmi remembered Sun Tzu's quote. Diksha was tasked with writing quote of the day on the office white board every morning, and Rashmi would skip reading it most of the time. But she found this quote powerful, and it stuck in her mind. She smiled and nodded.

"Hopefully, our seller account will go live in a few hours," Akshay said. "And when it will, we'll have an entire new world opened in front of us. The world which our enemy rules. It's going to be the best place to know about our enemy."

Striker 1 got activated in a few hours.

"What's up with this name?" Rashmi asked Akshay.

Akshay blushed. "I was a Counter-Strike freak in the college. My username was Striker 1. It was given by my girlfriend."

"You've a girlfriend?" She asked with a genuine surprise. "You never told me." She reminded herself that she'd never asked anything personal about her employees.

"Ex-girlfriend. We broke up long ago."

"Oops," she said and got back to Indiparadise. She had never been into a relationship. She wasn't very good with relations, anyway.

Akshay suggested her to study the forum section, as that was the place where Alphalion interacted with his fellow sellers. There were a variety of topics on the Indiparadise forum, spanning over more than fifty pages.

She was going through each and every post meticulously, reading Alphalion's comments and writing her observations on him in her notebook.

Alphalion seemed to an expert in computer programming and also in cryptocurrencies. He was a no-nonsense person, keeping his conversations restricted to work. Another peculiar thing Rashmi noted was that he would always address the group as 'Guyzz'. He would invariably start his comments with 'Guyzz', type it with the same spelling in all of his comments.

These observations, however, weren't yielding anything substantial. But habitually, she copied everything relevant into her notebook.

She stumbled upon a post that caught her attention. Indiparadise had increased their commission charges, and the low-volume sellers were the affected the most. One seller named 'Cocaman' started a new post speaking against Indiparadise and calling for other sellers to boycott the website until the admin reversed the revised commission charges. Cocaman even threatened Alphalion that if he wouldn't revoke his decision, Cocaman might drive the buyers offline and sell at even cheaper rates. Many sellers joined Cocaman and hurled similar threats.

Alphalion didn't heed the threats and dropped a single line comment. "You all have to face dire consequences."

Chapter 68

Nothing was going right in Diksha's life. It had been more than half a year that she'd been working with Pi Agency, but she never felt she was doing anything productive here, compared to what her boss and colleague, Akshay, were doing.

Boss would always tell her that she was equally important to the agency, but she knew she wasn't adding any value to the organisation. And now that the case had tilted towards cybercrime, it had gone beyond her purview. She wasn't a tech student, nor did she ever have any interest in information technology. She lost motivation, and she was losing interest in her job, in Pi Agency. And to top it all, her father's health was deteriorating, the reason being his daughter wasn't ready to marry.

She dialled her mother. "How's Dad?"

"Doctor had to give him insuling injection last night."

"God." Her father was a diabetic, but he had never had to take insulin injections.

"This morning he asked me if you're willing to meet that guy who lives in Delhi."

Not again. "Do you want me to?"

"I just want you to be happy," her mother said. "That's the reason I fought with your dad to send you to Delhi. If you're happy with your job, so be it. I'll speak to your dad. You don't need to meet that guy."

"I don't know, mom. Look what he's doing to himself."

Her mother sighed. "You know how old school he is. Plus his brothers and sisters would pester him against you. You remember how did they sensationalise that photo of you in a short dress, holding a wine glass at your friend's party?"

"That's why I blocked them all."

"And you know how unnecessary attention they give to their siblings? But don't worry. I'll manage. Focus on your job."

Diksha bit her lips. If she would refuse to meet this guy, there would be another argumenet between her parents, and Dad would worsen his health all the more. "Give me his number, mom. I'll contact him and meet him soon."

Chapter 69

"Befriend Alphalion," Rashmi instructed Akshay. "Make a list of all the rebellious sellers and send it to him. Suggest him to block their accounts."

Akshay nodded, with his head buried in his diary, as he noted Rashmi's instructions. He had been scolded by her in the past for not writing down instructions and observations, and he had implemented it the very next day.

"Make yourself an associate. A confidant."

Akshay raised his head, his eyebrows curving up.

"Tell him to make some changes in his website. Offer him to do it for him, infact."

Akshay jotted everything down.

Rashmi squeezed his forehead. Alphalion stared back to her from the screen. If he had been this close to her physically, she would have grabbed him by the neck and got him to sing. But he was not. He was just a username. The enemy is so close, yet so far. This awkward restlessness tormented her very being.

*

Akshay pinged Alphalion with the list of rebellious sellers, telling him that these people could pose serious security threat to the website. He received an uninterested response from Alphalion—"Okay, I'll look into it."

Over the course of next ten days, as planned, he suggested Alphalion minor changes in the website's outlook.

"Sounds good" Alphalion wrote back. "But I just don't have enough hands to do it."

"I can do it for you," Akshay replied as Striker 1. "Of course, in exchange for some Bitcoins."

Akshay had taken a gamble by asking for compensation. There was a chance of finding out the identity of Alphalion if he transferred the funds electronically. "Okay," Alphalion agreed.

Damn, Akshay thought. He submitted the codes to him nevertheless. Alphalion seemed impressed and started getting more involved with him.

"Are you a coder?" Alphalion wrote once.

Akshay concocted a backstory that he'd gotten a diploma in software engineering, but could not get a job, so he had to work in a sugar mill. Associating with Indiparadise was actually a compulsion to work within his livelihood.

Alphalion seemed to be moved by his story, and gave him more coding work. Akshay kept the records of all the Bitcoin transactions, as he was earning it from an illegal source and would have to declare it in his testimony when the time came.

Simultaneously, Akshay made a list of his observations on Alphalion in his notepad. Alphalion, as his boss had also observed, was an expert in programming. Akshay also steered the conversation from English to Hindi to judge Alphalion's origins. Alphalion could speak very well in Hindi, which meant he could be from the Hindi-speaking belt. He also used some North Indian slangs, like *Banda* (fellow), *vella* (jobless), *bathere* (plenty), *Khadd Ja* (stop or wait). This narrowed down his origina to Delhi, Haryana, or Punjab.

"There's no monsoon this year in Delhi," Akshay wrote.

"Right." Alphalion replied. "Climate change. Summers are getting hotter and longer here. "

That was a big clue for Akshay. Alphalion might be based out of Delhi.

Akshay presented his findings to boss.

"Keep going," his boss said. "We need to make him commit more such minute mistakes."

Boss never seemed content with anything. She had every reason not to be. They were still unclear on how exactly they were going to take Alphalion down.

Chapter 70

Even after gathering so many clues and observation on Alphalion, Rashmi didn't reach anywhere. *It's like running on a treadmill. You sweat, you pant, you burn calories, but you still remain where you'd started.* It was all over CBI exams again. Despite so much of hard work and dedication and determination, the end result was zero. It seemed failure loved to stick around her. Or she loved to stick around it. She wondered if she would cross the finishing line ever in her life. She was just meant to be a mediocre.

Her father stared back at her in all the photographs. Smile on his face, but pain in his eyes. A man failed by his wife and his daughter. His wife broke his family and his daughter broke his dream.

Her mother's words echoes in her ears. *"You're doomed, girl."* She closed her eyes. *"You're doomed, girl."*

"Shut up," she whispered.

Doomed.

She got up and pulled the thick curtain to bar the street light pouring in through the windows.

She slouched back on the couch. She couldn't see the Wall of Memories now. Now her mother could scream no more.

After a few moments, her phone lit up. The photographs came back to life. She clenched her jaws. She hated phone calls when she was brooding.

The screen flashed Sabrina.

It was ten past ten. *Why is she calling me at this hour?*

"Rashmi," Sabrina hushed. "I've got something to share."

"What?"

"Come to my place. I've got something related to Indiparadise."

*

Over the course of last thirty-four minutes, Rashmi did the worst driving of her life. She didn't bother parking her car, left it right on the road and headed straight for Sabrina's house.

She clomped up the stairs, climbing two steps at a time. As she reached the door, she thumped it until Sabrina opened the door.

"What's it?" Rashmi asked as soon as Sabrina appeared at the threshold.

Sabrina seemed to understand that Rashmi's patience had become thin as a metal leaf. She rushed back to the coffee table and picked a stack of what looked like envelopes. She passed it to Rashmi. "You told me about this envelope."

Rashmi studied the envelope. It was the same yellow envelope with a green leaf logo at the top corner.

"I got a delivery this evening," Sabrina said. "I don't know who sent it."

"You got it here, at Ankit's house."

"Yes. When I got it today, I suddenly remembered that we had received these envelopes a few times in our office as well. Ankit then used to courier it to someplace else."

Rashmi's mind raced. "The envelope is an Indiparadise branded packaging. I bet the sellers receive it from a central source. And that could be the owner himself. Alphalion wouldn't want risk giving this job to another seller."

"You remember you couriered these once when you were working with us," Sabrina said.

Rashmi squinted, racking her brain. Her head shook as if her neck joint had been rusty since a long time. "I'd shipped a lot of couriers to multiple destinations."

"I remember vaguely the place. It was, I guess, some place in Manesar. But I can't recall the exact addrees."

"I remember we used to file the tracking slips."

Sabrina nodded in small whooshes.

"The file is still in the office?"

Sabrina winced. "Yes."

"You've got the key card."

Sabrina eyes twinkled. "Let's roll."

Chapter 71

Before leaving for Pigeon Delivery's corporate office, Rashmi called Brajesh Arya and asked for his bodyguards. The security at Pragati Tower might prohibit them from entering at this hour and they might need the bodyguards' help.

The lone security guard at the entrance recognised Sabrina. Sabrina gave the pretext that that she'd some belongings left in the office that she just remembered. She was leaving back for Russia and has come to retrieve her belongings. The security guard allowed them to enter, but his evaluative gaze remained glued to Rashmi and the bodyguards.

The elevator was out of order. Rashmi turned to the staircase and darted up.

As she reached the fifth floor, she turned back and realised the bodyguards where still catching up. They reached after a minute, catching their breath. Sabrina was the last one to arrive.

Rashmi tapped the key card on the lock. The lock beeped but the frosted glass door didn't open. She turned back to Sabrina.

Sabrina grimaced. She pointed at mortise lock at bottom of the glass door. "Ankit used to lock the office by a secondary lock. Only he had the keys."

Rashmi winced, cursing under her breath.

"Wait." Sabrina disappeared into the hallway.

After a full half a minute of muted interval, Sabrina hobbled back with a fire extinguisher. She passed it to one of the bodyguards as soon as she neared her. The bodyguard caught the cylinder just before Sabrina could drop it.

"The honour is yours," Sabrina said.

The bodyguard's uncertain gaze shifted from Sabrina to Rashmi. Rashmi stepped away from the door.

The bodyguard smashed the cylinder on to the door. Two bangs and the frosted glass shattered into beads.

"Oi," the security guard called out from the ground floor.

Footsteps began to pound the stairs.

Rashmi jumped across the remaining glass and accessed the office. She switched on the main MCV switch and lit up the office. She riffled through the shelf in the main office. Leave record, Purchase Orders record, Invoices record, there was everything except the Shipping record.

She went back to the reception and pulled the drawer. There it was. The green file a handwritten label – Shipping record.

"What's happening here?" The security guard peered through the broken door. "I'm calling the cops."

One of the bodyguards grabbed him by his collar and pulled him inside the office. "If you do anything like that, you'll meet the same fate as this glass door."

"I'll lose my job," the guard whimpered.

"We'll get it changed before morning." The bodyguard motioned to the other to make a call to his boss.

Rashmi opened the file and sifted through the records. She accessed the slips of the period when she'd worked here. Manesar – she found the address on the tracking slip. She tore the slip out of the file. She held it in front of her face and read the address.

Chapter 72

Manesar was a village-turned-industrial town in the Gurgaon district of the Indian northern state of Haryana. It was a hub of some leading automobile manufacturers like Maruti Suzuki and Honda Motorcycles, and several other ancillary industries. It also housed the headquarters of India's special force unit, National Security Guards.

Rashmi drove further south west of his house in South Delhi on the Delhi-Jaipur highway, crossed Gurgaon City, and reached Manesar. She didn't have the exact location on Google Maps, but she knew once she was nearby, she could ask someone about intended address.

After moving out of Delhi by fifty-odd kilometres, she left the highway and took a slip road. There were fields all around, with occasional houses of farmers in between. As expected, and as planned, she asked a few people, and obtained the exact location of the address.

As she reached the place in question, she parked her car at a safe distance and observed. The house appeared to be a farmhouse. The windows were all sealed. There weren't any houses nearby, except for a tea shop. She waited to see any movement in the house.

A couple of hours passed, and no one came out from the house; nobody went inside, either. She spent another hour, but nothing changed. She began to doubt if anyone lived there. She had initially thought of going there posing as a wayward character, but it was too risky. Everything would be undone if Alphalion felt even a shadow of a doubt. But now, she had to confirm whether anyone lived there.

She got down and went to the tea stall. She ordered a tea and asked the vendor, "*Bhaiya,* I'm looking for a farmhouse here. I see this one a good option. Do you know who the owner is?"

"I don't know about the owner, ma'am," the vendor said.

"So no one lives here?"

"A caretaker lives here, but he seldom leaves the house. God knows what he does inside all day."

Caretaker. "How old is the guy?"

The vendor gave her a weird look, and she understood that wasn't the sort of question she should have asked. "Never mind. I'll look up the owner's contact info. Thanks."

Rashmi waited there till evening, but didn't see the 'caretaker'. The sun lowered down the western horizon and finally called it a day. The tea vendor, too, finished his day, but Rashmi remained persistent. She had done this boring investigation several times in the past. Criminals are nocturnal.

She waited on tenterhooks till midnight, but nothing happened. She finally turned the keys and drove away.

*

Rashmi reached Manesar the next morning at five. She parked her vehicle further away from her yesterday's spot. There was still an hour left for sunrise. It had rained last night and the unique smell of damp grass clogged the surroundings.

After an hour, birds began their cheerful carol, the first light of the morning cutting the darkness. It seemed someone had spilled the buckets of yellow and orange paints on the canvas of the morning sky.

A guy on a moped passed by her car and stopped in front of the house. Rashmi snatched the monocular.

He was holding translucent cotton bags in his hands. The bags contained groceries like milk, tea bags, snacks, veggies. The grocery guy entered through the main gate. He reached till the veranda and rang the bell.

The door wasn't visible from this angle. To see the person emerging from the door, she had to be right at the entrance gate. Damn.

Chapter 73

The morning's proceedings encouraged Rashmi to extend her surveillance beyond midnight. But apart from what she'd found in the morning, the rest of the day went exactly like the previous one. She repeated the same activity the next day as well. On the third day, she concluded that the caretaker of the farmhouse would come out of the house only once—to take the daily groceries at seven.

She sought an appointment from Brajesh Arya and dropped by his office while returning from Manesar. It was post office hour and all the employees had left the office. Brajesh Arya's secretary accompanied Rashmi to the office, guided her the way to Brajesh Arya's cabin, and left.

Brajesh Arya was standing along a large glass window, staring outside. He turned back as Rashmi entered.

Rashmi walked across the office and joined him. The glass window faced the national highway which had taken her to Manesar. The vehicles cruising on the highway were faintly visible. All she could see was her own reflection on the glass panel that was staring back at her.

"This window offers a good view of the skyline in the daytime," Brajesh Arya said.

"And hides the very existence of the entire world in the night," Rashmi said. *One way glass is a great leveller*, she thought. *It makes you invisible in the daylight and exposes you in the dark.*

Brajesh Arya shrugged. "You wanted to share something important."

She explained him how she found the address of the farmhouse in Manesar and she suspected the person living there was Alphalion.

"Great," Brajesh Arya said. "Let's go there with my bodyguards and grab that bastard."

"I want to do this more comprehensively," Rashmi offered.

Brajesh Arya reacted with narrowed eyes.

"Alphalion might not just be one man. He could be just the face of Indiparadise. But we know how he has eradicated Ankit Malik and Karan Shukla out of his way with such an ease when he felt they were detrimental to his business. He is surely backed up by the people who are capable of doing it. If we do what you are suggesting, we might end up with another Ankit Malik and Karan Shukla situation."

"So what do you suggest?"

"Look at these glasses Mr. Arya," Rashmi said. "You don't know if anyone is watching you from outside, because you can't see him. That's what I want to do with Alphalion. Catching him off guard; red-handed—as Alphalion," She gave a dramatic pause. "And in front of the police."

Brajesh Arya's eyes remained wide open.

"I know you've avoided getting the cops in right from the beginning. But we got to involve cops now."

Brajesh Arya looked back to the glass window again, staring his own reflection for long.

"Once Alphalion gets into the hands of the police," Rashmi said, "they will get everything out of him. They have the resources to end the entire Indiparadise Empire."

Brajesh Arya contemplated for a while and said, "But how will you accomplish it?"

"I have a plan. We just need to execute it cleanly."

"And how about bringing the police into the picture?"

Rashmi exhaled. "It would be difficult, but not impossible. You just need to file an FIR against Indiparadise."

*

Rashmi connected with Inspector Mohit Sherawat before leaving Brajesh Arya to file an FIR. She requested his help in catching the guy who was a suspect for running an online retail drug portal.

"You are still on this case," Inspector Mohit said. "I told you to stay away from these drug cases."

"Many things are happening right under your nose, Mohit, and you aren't even aware of them," Rashmi responded. "Even if the police are aware, they aren't doing anything."

"So you're a vigilante," Mohit jeered.

"No, I am not. I'm an investigator. I will share all the evidence with you which I've obtained during the course of my investigation. And I have a deal for you as well. You just need to act as I suggest."

Chapter 74

"How's your 'friendship' with Alphalion going?" Rashmi asked Akshay.

She stood in front of the white board. She'd shot up an arrow from Professor Vishwas Puri's name and had written 'Yellow envelope + Green lead logo'. From there, she'd drawn another arrow up, 'Sabrina: Envelope supply to Manesar'.

"It's more of friendship with benefits." Akshay chuckled. "He keeps on giving me occasional programming-related jobs. He is quite reserved. He only talks when I ask him something."

"Okay. The day has come to make use of this relationship." She put the tip of the marker on 'Manesar' and shot the arrow straight up to 'Alphalion'.

A chill coursed up Akshay's spine, his pulse jumping in sharp peaks.

Rashmi explained the plan.

*

"Buddy, I have important info for you," Akshay, as Striker 1, wrote to Alphalion.

"???" Alphalion responded.

"You remember I shared the list of rogue sellers? These sellers are now planning something big."

"Is it? Let's see what they can do."

"It's pretty serious. They have hired a team of hackers and are planning to hack your Bitcoin account. If I've heard the truth, they'll siphon off thousands of Bitcoins within a matter of a few days."

"How do you know all this?"

"I have been invited to their meetings."

"You want me to look into the security?" Alphalion responded after a few minutes.

"I want you to take care of these guys. It seems they have some *faadu* hackers this time."

"Just tell me who they are. I will handle them."

"I am finding everyone's real identity. I will share it with you at seven tomorrow morning," Akshay typed and hit the Enter key.

"Okay."

*

"Do you think he will come online tomorrow?" Akshay asked Rashmi after finishing his chat with Alphalion.

"He should. He must," Rashmi said. "It's a matter of money."

Chapter 75

"I'm considering resignation," Diksha said. She didn't come to office last week. Every time boss asked, she would say she was not well.

"Resignation," Akshay said. "Like leaving Pi Agency?"

"If that's what resignation means.

"For god's sake, Diksha, what is your problem? Not getting enough money?"

"It's not about money. I think I don't fit here."

"And what made you think so?" Akshay said. She was making him furious. The case had already bothered him enough.

"Because I couldn't do what you and boss do here. I wanted to do the same detective stuff here. I know I was hired for looking after marketing, but I wanted to be a detective, an investigator like you and Rashmi. But what I really do is stare at both of you during the meetings. I don't even exist to both of you."

Akshay gritted his teeth. He wanted to shout at her for being so foolish, but he realised she was right. They would never demand her participation. They were so involved in the work that they wouldn't even notice her sometimes. He calmed himself down and kept his hand on her shoulder. "Look, you have not even completed a year here. It's a learning stage for you. You will surely get work once you have gained enough experience."

"I can't wait that long. I'm seeing a guy today."

"Seeing a guy? For marriage?"

She nodded without looking at him.

It felt like his own heart stung him from inside. Diksha was getting married. It felt the same way he found out Smriti was dating someone else. Even worse. "Come on, this is not the right age for a marriage."

"Now you're going to teach me what's the right age for marriage."

Akshay felt like he was already losing Diksha. It was an odd feeling, he knew. But he couldn't help. Everything would end –

those discussions on Morning Quotes, leg pullings and cracking jokes, Golgappa outings. The office would nothing but a morgue without her. Please don't go. "I think you need to reconsider your decision. You can continue working here even after marriage."

"My parents still think that I work with that Ad agency," Diksha snapped. "If I tell the guy that I work for a private investigation agency, and I've lied to my parents about it, will he trust me? Will he trust a girl who's lied to her parents all along about her employment?"

"I don't know how these things work, but resignation is not the only way out. May be he would understand that you chose Pirvate Investigation as a career option."

"There's no other way out, Arora. I'll leave this. That way, I don't have to lie. Anyway, Rashmi Purohit doesn't need me."

"She needs both of us," Akshay exploded. "You were not there that day when her uncle was here. You don't know what he told me." Akshay narrated what their boss's uncle had told him, and in the heat of the moment, he told her about the letter he'd found in Rashmi's bookshelf. "She has a troubled past. She needs us. She wouldn't express it, but if I believe Mr. Purushottam Purohit, we must stand by her side—always."

Diksha stood her ground as a stone.

"I see my friends working with big-shot software MNCs," Akshay said, "and many have moved abroad. And I am sitting here in a small basement office with just one colleague. I used to feel that I should leave this job. My friends think of my job as a lowly job. 'Wow, being a detective is like a dream job,' they pretend in front of me and mock at my job behind my back. I stopped hanging out with them for this very reason. But then I think how many of them are hunting a criminal. How many of them are saving the life of a troubled college kid. How many are actually giving something back to the society? Pi Agency has trusted me, Rashmi Purohit has trusted me, and I am not going to run away when she and the agency need me the most. I am not selfish."

"I am not being selfish—"

"Yes, you are," Akshay cut in. "We're so close to crack this case."

"And what will happen after you find Alphalion. Rashmi Purohit will be famous. May be you, too, the sidekick of Rashmi

Purohit. But what about me? I'll stay the same. The unimportant and irrelevant employee of Pi Agency. I'm not being selfish, Arora, I'm being honest here."

"You are running away from your responsibilities. That's all I can say. But I cannot. I will not. If you think you will be happy leaving us, go ahead. We don't need cowards like you."

Chapter 76

Rashmi, along with Inspector Mohit and a handful of constables, reached Manesar at four in the morning. They parked their vehicle roughly five hundred meters away from Alphalion's hideout.

Rashmi had to catch Alphalion as Alphalion. Whoever was the man behind the mask of Alphalion, she had to catch him when he was present online as Alphalion, with his computer on. For that they needed to appear in his house right at the time he was online. They could have done it anytime in the day, when Alphalion was online, but given the fact there was only one visitor which came to his house during the entire day, if he found a visitor coming at any other time, he would certainly be suspicious.

That was the reason she had asked Akshay to keep the time to chat with Alphalion the next morning at seven, because that was the time when the grocery man came to his house, as he did every day, and that was the time he would be most casual and least alert.

At six-thirty, she noticed a moped heading toward the farmhouse. "Shit," she cursed. "That is the grocery man. Stop him."

The police party got into action and stopped the grocery man midway.

"*Kya hua*, sir?" the grocery man asked, his eyebrows lifted anxiously to form wrinkles on his forehead.

"Are you going to that house?" Mohit asked, pointing toward Alphalion's house.

"Yes," he confirmed. "I deliver groceries to his house every day."

"But why are you half an hour early today?" Rashmi asked.

"*Bhaiya* asked me to come early today. He said he has some work at seven."

"*Bhaiya* has some work at seven," Rashmi whispered to Mohit. "And Alphalion has a meeting with Akshay today at seven."

Mohit nodded, gesturing that he got Rashmi's drift.

Rashmi took her phone out and called Akshay. "Is he online?"

"Not yet, boss," Akshay spoke from the other end.

Rashmi turned toward Mohit. "We can't allow him to go right now. Alphalion is not online."

*

The grocery man's phone buzzed at six-forty-five a.m. "*Bhaiya* is calling," he said.

"Pick the call and put it on loudspeaker," Rashmi instructed him.

The grocery man followed the instructions without questioning.

"Where are you?" the voice from the other end said. The voice sounded familiar.

"*Bhaiya*, I…I am waiting for the milk van," grocery man faltered.

"I told you, I have an important work today," the voice barked. "Come now."

"Okay, *Bhaiya*. I am coming." The grocery man looked at Rashmi helplessly.

She called Akshay again. Before she could say 'Hello', Akshay said, "He is not online, yet."

Damn, she cursed under her breath. "We have to wait."

*

Exactly at seven, Rashmi received Akshay's call.

"Boss, he's online now."

Everyone got back on their feet. They hid behind the front boundary wall of the house. "Is he online now?" Rashmi asked Akshay.

"Yes, Boss."

"Make sure he stays that way."

She gestured for the grocery man to enter through the main gate. Everyone else followed him deftly.

While the grocery man stood in the veranda in front of the door, everyone took their guns in their hands were ready to barge into the house.

"Is he online?" Rashmi whispered on the call.

"Positive."

She gestured for grocery man to ring the bell when she got a positive response from Akshay.

The grocery man pushed the doorbell. She heard footsteps approaching toward the door. The door opened. "I told you to come early today."

Rashmi recognised the voice. She might be wrong. She had to confirm by seeing his face.

The very next moment, Rashmi and the policemen appeared behind the grocery man. "Hello, Alphalion," Rashmi said.

Chapter 77

It took only half a heartbeat for Rashmi to recognise the chubby, acne filled face. The voice had already told her the identity of Alphalion, and only a glance was required to confirm her doubt.

Terror spread into Ankit Malik's chunky features as he saw Rashmi and the men in Khakis. He wasn't expecting them to be here. Neither had Rashmi expected to find him here. He was apparently killed by the Alphalion. But before Rashmi could analyse the situation, Ankit Malik turned around and darted back inside the house.

Rashmi understood what he was trying to do and chased him. She grabbed a handful of his T-shirt's collar. The T-shirt choked him from the other end. He stumbled forward and his T-shirt gave away. Rashmi wrapped her arm around his neck before he could get away.

"Bitch," Ankit Malik yelled. "You framed me."

"Mohit," Rashmi called out, "Get hold of his laptop. Don't shut the lid. Don't push any key. We'll lose everything." Rashmi had read in an article that cyber criminals often use an emergency encryption key. Whenever they would be on the brink of getting caught, they would hit the key and everything would disappear in the thin air. No one then could every prove that they did the crime. If Ankit Malik managed to hit the key, Alphalion was gone forever.

Ankit Malik punched on her ribs with his elbows. "Bitch. You bitch. You framed me."

Ankit swayed his head, his blubbery belly. He bent down at one moment and arched his back at another. Rashmi felt like she was tackling a mad bull by her bare hands.

The constable joined her and pinned him down. They then charged him with their wooden batons. "I'm not Alphalion," Ankit yelped, lying crumpled on the floor, covering his head with his hands. "She's framing me, officers. I'm not Alphalion."

*

Four days after Ankit Malik aka Alphalion was deposited to the custody, the forensic experts retrieved Rohan's video along with several other such videos from Indiparadise servers. The servers had been located in the same house. Indiparadise had been taken down the same day. Forensic experts then dug out details of all sellers and began to carry out raids.

"Thank you, ma'am," Rohan said. "Thank you for everything.

Brajesh Arya brought his son to her office today. He'd finally got the courage to tell his son that how he'd managed to bring their perpetrator down.

She gave a hearty smile. "Thanks to your dad who hired me at the first place. You've got a new life. I hope you'll do justice to it."

"I'll ma'am."

Brajesh Arya asked Rohan to go upstairs back to the car. After Rohan left, he said, "So Ankit Malik is Alphalion. It seems you weren't all wrong, Ms Purohit."

"I'm still not finding it convincing enough. I mean I've caught him red-handed, as Alphalion, but… but I don't know. He just doesn't seem to be the guy who could lie to you even after so much beating. If he was Alphalion, why he didn't tell you the truth that day itself?"

"May be the weak and meek Ankit Malik was a mask," Brajesh Arya said. "A mask to hide his true identity of Alphalion. He was an entrepreneur. He would do all in his capacity to hide his criminal avatar."

"And given who the owner of the house was, only a man like Ankit Malik could've been trusted with running the criminal website."

After police further investigated, they found that the house was registered in the name of Sunita Prabhakar – the dead wife of politician, Rishi Tanwar. The case was still under investigation until Ankit Malik spilled the truth to the police.

Sunita Prabhakar had invested initially in Pigeon Delivery. She had many such small businesses. Mostly IT works. She would take work with freelancers and fresh graduates. Ankit Malik revealed that Indiparadise was Sunita Prabhakar's brain child. But the lake of drug world was filled with crocodiles. She had strife with some of those guys. As a result—they killed her. But he still hadn't accepted that he was Alphalion. Whatever knowledge he had about Indiparadise and Sunita Prabhakar was obtained from Alphalion.

That was the reason she was not convinced with the conclusion. Perhaps Brajesh Arya was right. Perhaps Ankit Malik was a master liar. His lawyers would be teaching him to quote these statements. Perhaps the detective in her was being a paranoid.

Chapter 78

Diksha met Harshit Patel at a nearest Starbucks. He stood around six feet, a bit lesser, actually. He had a lean frame. His hair was cut smartly, sleek and held together by a hair gel. He came to meet her in a smart fit, sky blue button down shirt, tucked cleanly inside a lean fit black trouser. The cuffs had been folded up until the elbow, revealing a Kenneth Cole analogue watch.

When the girl at the counter called his and Diksha's name, he got up in a flash and collected their mugs.

"Here we go." Harshit put Diksha's coffee first on the table in front of her and then took his seat with his cup in his hand. "The company you work with," he said, taking the first sip, "it laid off many employees. Everything fine there now?"

Diksha nodded. "I think they'll kick me out soon. I'm searching for a new job, anyway."

"Yeah, you must. No point in working with a firm which hangs a sword above your neck all the time."

"What about you?" She feigned a smile. "I guess you're working for just a few years and will eventually join you dad's business."

Harshit chuckled. "That's what he tells everyone. He was expecting me to join his business after I completed MBA. I decided otherwise." He put his cup back on the table. "Being the son of a businessman, everyone expects me to follow my father's suit. He will make me the CEO in a few years, no doubt about that. But the expectations will always be there. That I'll have to become like him one day. And expectations are like a sword hanging over my neck. I can't do that. I'm happy with my job. I'm happy with whatever money I'm earning out of it."

Diksha remembered what Arora had told her about Rashmi. She, too, was supposed to follow her father's profession. Her father too had expectations with her which she couldn't achieve. Perhaps she didn't truly want that. She wanted something more. Pi Agency? May be.

They talked more about varying topics. About college life, movies, TV shows, holidays, job, the pros and cons of working with a start-up. Probably it was from there the topic of Indiparadise popped up.

"You heard about Indiparadise, right?" Harshit said. "The owner was running an online drug cartel surreptitiously. Can you imagine? An online marketplace for illegal drugs." He huffed. "These criminals won't leave anything."

"Alphalion is caught?" Diksha asked in utter surprise. Boss and Arora had finally managed to bust the website.

"That was Ankit Malik's alias. Yeah he's been caught by the police."

"Pi Agency," she said. "Pi Agency was working on that case?"

Harshit cocked his head. "What's that? Some special police team?"

"It's a private investigation firm."

Harshit shrugged. "No mention of any such agency in any of the news report I've read or watched."

Strange. She felt an urge to call Akshay and ask what had happened. Why there was no mention of Pi Agency?

She got up, grabbing her bag. "I've to go?"

"What?" Confusion flooded his face. "Where?"

She left without a response.

Chapter 79

*N*o, No. *it shouldn't have happened.*

On her way back to her home, Akshay had told her that excluding Pi Agency from the case was the part of the pact boss had done with her friend, Inspector Mohit Sherawat. Mohit had agreed to help Rashmi only if he was to take all the credits to himself.

She controlled her tears. Boss and Akshay worked so hard for this case. She, too, was involved in the case for a long time. And now all credit was taken by Mohit Sherawat. Pi Agency, even after busting a sinister online drug cartel, still remained a small-fry.

A reluctant tear escaped her mascara lined eye. *Strange.* She hated Pi Agency and Rashmi Purohit a few days ago. And now she was weeping for them.

She searched on YouTube for news on Indiparadise case.

Rishi Tanwar, husband of late Sunita Prabhakar – the mastermind behind Indiparadise – was jostling through the flock of journalists. "My wife is no criminal," he said, as his bodyguards were trying to keep the journalists away from him. "That man Ankit Malik is lying. He's trying to put all the blame to my late wife. He knew very well that she's not here to prove he's a liar."

Rishi Tanwar pushed the crowd away to walk away. He had two bodyguards— one was a hefty African national, and another was awfully tall – who manhandled the journalists.

"Hato," said the African. "No more questions." His voice sounded familiar. In fact, the duo looked familiar. "Get away," the African howled at the journalists.

His voice was eerily familiar. She had heard this voice quite recently. There was something peculiar about it. This was the same African-accented Hindi-speaking voice she had heard from the intruders who had attacked her and Akshay in the office.

She observed that the bodyguard had a similar built—bulky

and colossal. And the second guy was the same seven-footer. Shiver slithered up her spine. *Are these the same guys?*

That could be a mistake. They probably weren't the same guys, and the voice just sounded similar. But what if they were the same attackers?

Chapter 80

Marketing—that was all Diksha knew about, and that was what she'd learnt and applied in her brief professional career. And that was what she intended to find in her own way if Rashmi Purohit and Akshay Arora were correct in finding Alphalion. Or if they did something terribly wrong.

I'm not a coward, Arora.

"4 Ps of Marketing," she wrote on a sheet paper, and underlined it. Below the heading, she wrote, "Product, Price, Place, and Promotion."

These four were the basic parameters the marketing managers controlled to market their products. In her one year of experience in the previous firm, Diksha had applied extensively the four Ps of marketing, especially the last two Ps—Place and Promotion.

Place and Promotion were the critical factors for any business to present their product or service to the customer. She would work around these two variables to market the business of her employer. She believed the drugs business, after all, was a business, and the owners of Indiparadise would have needed the same marketing strategy to market their business.

The Place variable would determine where the product was required to be placed so that the intended customer would find it easily, and the promotion variable would decide how the product was promoted among the intended customers. Diksha would often blend these two variables to create an efficient marketing plan—promoting the product in the right places.

"What would be that place where Indiparadise would promote their business so that the intended customers would come to know about it?"

Indiparadise wasn't the kind of website for which the owners would go openly on social media and run a sponsored ad in front of the world. She recalled during her tenure at the last place that she would write good stuff about her company on the forums which were related to her employer's business so that the related customers would come across the info.

Indiparadise could have done the same, she thought.

The best place where the targeted customers visited would be the forums related to drugs.

She searched in Google with the keyword "Indiparadise," with an intention of looking into such forums. The results were overwhelming. It was going to take plentiful time to search through.

*

Diksha was awake the whole night, and slept only for a few hours in the morning. She got back to work again in the afternoon. Now she wasn't aware, nor did she care, what the time it was.

She stumbled upon an interesting comment in one of the forums related to cocaine: "Guyzz, I came across a new website called Indiparadise. It's like an Amazon of drugs; an Indian version of the famous Silk Road. There are a variety of drugs at cheap prices, delivered right at your doorsteps!" The comment ended with the Tor link for Indiparadise.

Guyzz. She remembered boss had told her and Akshay that Alphalion addressed people with Guyzz in his comments on Indiparadise.

This is Alphalion.

The post she just found was the oldest of all. She copied the comment and searched it on Google. Around the same period, she found exactly the same comment posted on various other forums. She checked the username of the person who had posted these comments.

Alphalion90. Her pulse quickened.

To cross-check her find, she noted the earliest date on which this comment was posted and searched on Google before that date. There were no results!

"Yes," her voice came out high-pitched. *This is one of the earliest posts from Alphalion.*

She remembered she'd noted a discrepancy on Indiparadise website pertaining to 'Guyzz', which she'd ignored when no one had asked for her participation.

She opened the Pi Agency Dropbox drive on her laptop and accessed the folder in which Arora had saved all the discussions on the seller forum.

Alphalion had seldom used the word Guyzz in any of the recent posts. Even if he'd used, it was simple Guys. She noted the date from which this change had happened. It was around the time when Ankit Malik was disappeared.

Her mind raced.

She picked up her phone and dialled her boss's number. "Ankit Malik is not Alphalion."

"Diksha, weren't you sick?" her boss asked.

"No…I mean, yes. I mean no…Ankit Malik is not Alphalion. I am coming to the office now."

"It's half past ten," Rashmi said.

Diksha checked the time and slapped her forehead. "I can't wait to tell you what I found. I am coming to the office."

Chapter 81

Diksha was setting up the projector when Akshay entered the office. His hair was messed up and his eyes were sleep deprived. "Did boss organise this meeting to persuade you not to resign?" he asked.

"Shut up, you coward," Diksha spat.

Akshay spread his hands.

"I called for this meeting," Diksha said.

"At this hour? You have seriously gone mad."

Rashmi stormed into the office with a mug of espresso and took her seat. "Diksha, I've never used expletives on you, but if something you found isn't worth organising a meeting at the middle of the night, you got to listen some choicest of abuses from me."

Akshay let out a chuckle. Diksha and boss both glowered at him.

Purushottam Purohit, too, descended down the stairs laboriously. "Do we have the success party going on? I prefer scotch and retro music."

Rashmi pressed her lips and turned to Diksha. "Did you invite Mr. Arya, too?"

Diksha stuck her tongue out. "I thought Purushottam uncle's expertise would be useful."

Before leaving for the office, Diksha had quickly made a PowerPoint presentation. She'd learnt from her previous boss that anything and everything must be presented in the form of a PowerPoint presentation. She had made a number of presentations in that few months of her employment, and by now, she had become expert in them.

She first explained how she'd implemented the marketing strategy of 4Ps to find a 'digital fingerprint' of Alphalion. She had taken the screenshots of all the comments she had found from the user Alphalion90, who had kept this username invariably the same throughout. She had also made list of all those websites in which Alphalion90 had posted that same comment.

"No one would copy-paste the same post on several forums," Diksha said, "in the same time period. I won't do that, no matter how much I would've loved something. Think about it. We don't take such pain." She turned back to pointed the laser on Alphalion90. "Unless I'm the owner of the business. These forums require the users to register with their email ID. They also store the IP address of the user as well. You know what I mean?"

Akshay raised his hand. "But that doesn't necessarily mean this Alphalion90 is associated with Indiparadise. Someone might have genuinely loved the site and posted about it."

"Fuck off," Diksha spoke under her breath, but Akshay just smiled back. *This guy's crazy.* "Okay. And what about Alphalion90? Why only Alphalion90? Another coincidence? I remember boss used to say something about coincidence."

Rashmi, who had been sitting there silently, spoke, "Guyzz with double 'z'—a word that Alphalion uses every time he addresses people on Indiparadise. So I accept Diksha's theory that this comment was posted by Alphalion. But this doesn't prove he isn't Ankit Malik."

Diksha waited for this question. She then explained her finding on Alphalion's comments on the seller forum. She showed them how Guyzz had changed to Guys. "You remember Brajesh Arya had said that everyone commits a rookie error in the beginning. This might be the rookie error that Alphalion had done."

"These websites," Akshay said, "wherever Alphalion90 has posted the comments, can't we ask them to share the email ID?"

Purushottam Purohit cleared his throat. "They can, but they won't."

Everyone turned their attention toward Purushottam.

"These websites are bound to protect your personal data," Purushottam said. "When we register with our email IDs on such forums, you would have seen a declaration by these websites: your information is safe with us. It comes under their privacy policy to protect PII, Personal Identifiable Information. They aren't going to share any user data with any stranger."

"Not even to the authorities?" Rashmi asked.

"Government has given the right to some authorities to ask for the PII of any user from these websites."

"That's the reason I called you to the meeting," Diksha said, smiling.

"It's not that simple," Purushottam said, looking back at her with a stern face. "Authorities would ask for such data only if they are investigating. As per the law, they require written documents. And even if I request any known person from a relevant authority to go out of their way, he would refuse. With so much fuss going on about right to privacy, I don't think anyone would want to get into trouble."

"So we don't have any option to find anything about this Alphalion90," Rashmi said.

"At least not through these forums," Puroshottam said coldly, holding the prints of the presentation. The page having the forums' list was opened.

Everyone got back to reading the presentation, unaware of what to do next.

Purushottam, too, read the list of websites again. He suddenly looked back at Rashmi, as if he'd found something.

He was about to say something when Rashmi stopped him, "I know. But that's not going to work."

"It will. She will definitely…" Purushottam paused and looked around. "I think we have got something to discuss."

"There is nothing to discuss, uncle," sharpness entered her tone. "I think that's all for today. I will see what else I can do to with this Alphalion90."

She shut her laptop's lid and walked out. Purushottam Purohit followed her.

Diksha turned to Akshay to ask if he'd any idea about what happened, but she found Akshay was already up close to her. Much to her shock, he hugged her.

"Arora," she said, pushing his muscular body away. "What are you doing?"

He disengaged her. It was the first time a guy hugged her. She could still the shiver coursing through her veins.

"You nailed it, girl," he said. "I'm so glad. And I'm happy you're back."

"Any idea what's just happened?"

"I think I know. Let's go upstairs.

Chapter 82

Rashmi climbed up to her house and shut the door behind her. Her heart was pounding. She hadn't expected that her uncle would remember the name of her estranged mother's company, 'weanswer.com'—one of the forums on which Alphalion90 had posted about Indiparadise two years ago.

She had seen the name in the list last as soon as it was on the screen and it had immediately roused her temper.

As soon as she saw her uncle noticing this website, she knew he would come up with a proposition to approach this website for Alphalion90's credentials; approaching her mother. She would rather die than ask her mother for help.

You're doomed, girl.

"What happened to you?" Purushottam entered the house. "I was just suggesting that—"

"I know what you were trying to suggest. I am not going to her. That's out of the question."

Purushottam dropped his shoulders. "Down there, that kid Diksha, she did all this for Pi Agency. For you, so that you could get to the bottom of the truth. Don't do it for yourself, do it for those kids. They respect you a lot. They love you, actually. Don't let your ego get the better of you."

"It's not about my ego," Rashmi shot back. "It's about my father's dignity; your elder brother's dignity. I don't want to see myself begging before that woman who left my father alone. It was because of that woman that my family broke, my father died." *You're doomed, girl.* "And no matter what, I am not going to her at any cost."

Purushottam Purohit sighed. His eyes travelled from her to the Wall of Memories. The happy moments, the cheerful memories. Everything was ruined; just because of a single, selfish act of her mother. How was she supposed to ask for help from the same person who'd destroyed her family?

Someone cleared his throat at the door. It was Akshay. "I…I

am sorry, boss…" Akshay stuttered, standing fixed at the door. Diksha was peering in from behind. "I have no right to intervene in your private discussion, but I…I need to tell you something."

"What?" Rashmi snapped. She wasn't interested in entertaining Akshay at this moment.

Much to her and her uncle's surprise, Akshay entered and walked straight to the bookshelf.

He stopped and turned toward her. "I am sorry, boss. I shouldn't have done this, but…" He drew a book from the shelf—*The Story of my Experiment with Truth*.

"It was my father's favourite book," Rashmi said.

"I picked this book the night I stayed here, I don't know why, may be just out of curiosity, and…" Akshay flipped the pages and plucked out an envelope. "And I found this."

Rashmi took the envelope from Akshay slowly, without displaying any expression, as always.

"It was sealed," Akshay said, "so I assume you hadn't ever opened it, or didn't know that it existed."

She opened the envelope and took out the note.

Chapter 83

Beta,

This is something unusual I am doing here—writing a letter to you! I haven't ever written any letters to you, not even a text message. But what I want to say here couldn't be told in person. Actually, I don't have the courage to talk to you about this in person.

When you were born, your mother and I had decided that you would be our only child, so that we could put all our attention only on you, so that we can give our best to you. Right from the start, I wanted you to become a CBI officer like me. Yes, it was my dream.

As you grew up, I saw more of myself in you, and my dream of seeing you as a CBI officer grew stronger every day. But we do not always get what we wish for. Not all dreams get fulfilled. I know you tried hard, but sometimes, things just don't go our way. I accept that I was disappointed. It would not be fair if I hid it from you. It was natural. But it was also apparent to me that you didn't just want to do what everyone else was doing. You wanted something more from yourself, and your life. You didn't just want to become like your father. You wanted more. And that's when Pi Agency happened.

I didn't like the idea of you becoming a private investigator, let alone owning an agency. But later, I realised you are doing what even I could never have imagined. Getting a job, be it private or with the government, demands hard work, but what you are doing requires courage.

I have now understood that building Pi Agency means true success for you. And in your success lies my happiness. We all know that success needs passion and determination, but the most important thing we chose to ignore is that success, before everything, demands sacrifice. Success for your mother meant becoming an entrepreneur, and she had to sacrifice her family for that. I was hurt when she left me. I hated her for that.

Move on — two words, and order that must be followed, but which requires you to turn to stone from inside.

So I moved on. Forgiving someone doesn't mean you have accepted defeat. Your mother was right in her own way, and so are you. For you to be successful, you and me both have to sacrifice my dream, for your dream will take you to a better place in life.

Now you know why I wrote this letter to you? We have never had such conversations, such emotional talks. I don't know if I would ever be able to share this letter with you. I hope when I am gone, which seems it may happen soon, you will see this letter and understand.

You have not let me down, beta. You are doing a brilliant job with Pi Agency. All the effort you are putting in is worth it.

Wishing you very best for Pi Agency, and life.

Papa.

Chapter 84

Rashmi folded the note and closed her eyes. Her father's letter was by her side all these years, inside his favourite book which he would always ask her to read. Each word in this letter rang in her ears in her father's voice. She glanced at the Wall of Memories. She regretted of not talking to him about her mother, about not getting into CBI, about Pi Agency. There were a lot of things they could've talked about. She could've involved him in Pi Agency. May be that could've given his father some motivation to live more.

She maintained the frigid look on her face, but the emotional ebullitions inside betrayed her. A stream of tear trickled down through the edges of her closed eyelids. She moved her face away from everyone. She still was conscious enough to hide her emotions from others.

"I shouldn't have read it," Akshay said, "and I thought of sharing it with you once the case was over. But when I listened to your conversation just now, I felt you must read it. I am sorry, but I think your father was right."

"I need some time alone," Rashmi said. "Please leave."

Purushottam put his hand on Akshay's shoulder, gesturing for him to leave. They quietly walked out of the house. Their expressions, however, suggested that they didn't want to. They looked worried for her.

All along, Rashmi felt that her father had thought of her job as lowly and menial. She regretted that she couldn't fulfil his dreams. But she was wrong. Her father had never expressed his feelings to her, the same issue she'd probably inherited from him, but now, through this letter, he had. He, too, wanted to see Pi Agency reach the pinnacle of success. And it was now up to her to accomplish it. She opened the Chrome browser in her mobile and typed, "weanswer.com."

*

The security guard stopped Rashmi's car as she was entering a business park located in Noida. A part of the National Capital region, Noida, a satellite city like Gurgaon, was a well-organised city and a part of the Indian state of Uttar Pradesh. After she had found the contact details of her mother's firm, she sought for an appointment with the owner itself, Ms Madhu Trivedi. The secretary didn't entertain her at first, saying that Madhu Trivedi wasn't free until next month. Rashmi, however, insisted to mention her name to Madhu Trivedi. After a while, the secretary called back, informing her that the meeting had been arranged for the next morning.

After the security check, Rashmi drove her car down to the basement parking, and headed to the office, which was on the sixth floor.

"It's been a long time, beta!" Madhu walked cheerfully toward Rashmi and hugged her as she entered Madhu's office.

Rashmi's hands, however, remained at her side.

"I knew you would come to meet me some day," Madhu said as she released her from her embrace. "Have a seat. What would you like to have?"

"Nothing. I have come here for some work."

Madhu waited to hear her out, a smile on her face.

Rashmi straightaway explained the case she was dealing with, and what she needed from her.

Madhu wasn't smiling anymore; she seemed to be brooding.

"You are thinking about the privacy policy, right?" Rashmi said.

Madhu nodded.

"So you can't help me."

"I never said that." A weird smile appeared on Madhu's face. "I was just remembering the day when I came to your office years ago."

Rashmi was expecting that her mother would surely bring up this topic.

"I was trying to remember what you said that day."

Rashmi remembered clearly what she'd said that day.

"You know, beta," Madhu said, "this world is a small place. What goes around comes around."

Rashmi felt sudden pangs of humiliation inside. She wanted to get up and leave this place without wasting another moment.

But she controlled her temper. She waited for a moment to regain her calmness and said, "Is it possible for you to share the email id?"

"Of course," Madhu said. She looked like she had won a battle. She made a call, and after a few minutes, a guy came with a Post-it note.

"Alphalion90's credentials, as you asked, ma'am. It's an old ID, and it hasn't been active for more than a year or so." He set the note in front of Madhu and left.

"For you." Madhu slid the paper toward Rashmi. "It's against our company policy to give the PII of a user. But you are my daughter." She paused for a dramatic effect. "Yes, you may not consider me your mother, but you are still my daughter."

Rashmi picked the paper and folded it once, without even looking at the email ID. "Thanks. Got to leave now. I have a lot of work to do." She stood up and turned to leave.

"By the way, my proposal is still on the table," Madhu said. "Come and join me. Leave that *worthless* agency. I don't even remember its name. You will earn ten times more here."

Worthless. Rashmi smiled bitterly. She turned back with the same smile.

Madhu stared back at her with confusion.

"That's the difference between Papa and you. You look down upon everything. Everything looks lowly to you in comparison to your job and your career. I hated you for leaving Papa. But today, I want to thank you for leaving him. You never understood him. And you never deserved to be with him."

Chapter 85

The email ID itself gave away the name of Alphalion. Countless people could be of same name, but this particular name was the name of a person who had been closely associated with Rohan. However, it was hard for her to swallow that this guy was Alphalion. She checked this ID on Facebook, Twitter, Instagram, LinkedIn, and everywhere found the same guy.

How can you be Alphalion? And why?

When she went on to check his PG, she found that he had gone somewhere and it had been over a month. She remembered Karan Shukla, too, had said that he would disappear for months, doing some freelancing work for unknown people. He also told her that time that his father was a widower and lived in Laxmi Nagar.

Posing as an employer, Rashmi dialled the college's admin's number, and successfully gleaned his residential address mentioned in the records. It was in Laxmi Nagar.

Laxmi Nagar was located at the east corner of Delhi. It would take Rashmi an hour to travel from South Delhi to East Delhi. She was aware of the narrow streets of Laxmi Nagar and the kind of skills required manoeuvring the vehicle in such conditions. She preferred taking the metro to Laxmi Nagar instead.

After she alighted at Laxmi Nagar, she had to ask a few people to reach the address, which was located, as she had expected, in an uncapacious street. The houses, which were three to four stories tall, appeared as if they had been stuffed inside the streets. However, if one was to buy any of these houses, the money he would have to funnel out from his bank accounts was no less than ten million rupess.

She read the Surname on the name plate. She'd reached the correct location. She pressed the doorbell. The house was fronted by a black, wrought iron gate. She peered through the gate. There was a small porch, followed by the main wooden door of the house.

A middle-aged man emerged through the door. "Yes?" the balding man asked as he opened the gate.

"Hello, uncle. I want to have a word with you."

"What's the matter?"

"It's about your son. I am from his college."

"He doesn't live here anymore," the old man said.

"Oh! Can you share his current address?"

"I don't know where he lives now," he said gruffly.

The relationship between the father and son appeared to be a strained one. But who was she to judge? She didn't have a sound relationship with her mother, either. "It's about his job. It's kind of important."

He looked thoughtful. "Come in."

Rashmi followed him inside the house. "Your son has put a lot of people into deep trouble. I don't know how long he's going to survive." She narrated her everything that had happened in the past few months.

"No, my son cannot do that." His eyes reflected grief, furrows cascaded on his forehead.

"I know it's hard to digest for you. After all, he's your son. But I've all the evidence that say he's a criminal."

"He was ambitious," he said, his eyes resting on the ceiling. "He considered himself special. He wanted to become an entrepreneur, start a business of his own. He wasn't interested in studies. He wanted money from me to start his own business. I told him I was just a government school teacher who was left with a few years of job. And he moved out. He said he got some freelancing job with big people, some important guy. I knew he was lying, but I didn't stop him. At least he was looking to live independently. Little did I know that…" he trailed off and broke into sobs.

Rashmi had no idea how to comfort crying people. "You can still help him, uncle."

He looked at her, wiping his tears. "Call him, and tell him as I say."

After over forty-minutes Alphalion's father called him and told, as she'd instructed, that some strangers at his house and they would do him harm if his son wouldn't come here within an hour, Rashmi heard a sharp honking in the street. He seemed to be in a great hurry, as she'd expected.

The sound of the revving engine stopped right in front of the gate. The iron gate opened and banged with the cement wall. Footsteps approached the door.

The wooden door slammed open and Adi Luthra barged inside.

Chapter 86

Rashmi stood on the edge of the terrace, her hands resting on the iron railings. The street four floors below was lively with children playing a game of cricket. But up here, it was calm and serene. A flock of birds were returning to their home. The sky's shade had turned a bit darker. The air today was cool and pleasant.

Adi Luthra stood next to her, staring into the distance. When he'd entered the house, his father hugged him and cried for a long time. Then he had several questions for him. Adi asked him to wait and took Rashmi to the terrace as he didn't want to speak with her in front of his father.

He didn't say a word after coming up on the terrace. The silence had stretched quite long.

"I knew you would come one day," Adi broke the silence. "I knew it the day I met you. I saw the fire in your eyes. I don't know for what reason, but it's there."

"Trying to flatter me?" she said.

Adi smiled wryly.

"Why did you do it, Adi? Why did you do it to your friend? You know what could've happened to Rohan if that video was out. He could've fallen into depression. He already had, actually. Worse, he could've killed himself."

"I was helpless," Adi said, still staring into the sky, the retreating birds. "I started all this for money, but I didn't know it would turn ugly."

"Tell me from the beginning."

Adi ran both his hands across his hair and let out a deep exhale from his mouth. "I worked for Sunita Prabhakar's software business, and I was doing quite well. She thought of me as a bright kid. She even introduced me to his husband. I impressed him as well, thinking that he would help me get into a government job. But I was wrong. Rishi Tanwar had different plans. He wanted me to set up for him an Indian version of Silk Road – Indiparadise.

When I refused, he threatened me with dire consequences. He made me create the website and handle it as Alphalion. He then asked me to market this website on the internet on portals and forums related to drugs. That's where I committed the mistake, by using my own email ID."

Rookie error. She remembered Diksha.

"I knew some day police will find who Alphalion is, and when they would, it would be I who would be booked. Police could never touch a politician of the stature of Rishi Tanwar. So I told everything to Sunita Prabhakar. Sunita Prabhakar confronted her husband, threatened to tell everything to the police. Tanwar got away with her by poisoning her food.

"I'd no other choice but to continue. Tanwar made me fall my friend Rohan into drug addiction and then made his video and blackmail his father. Tanwar then used the extortion money to fund the start-ups, the likes of Ankit Malik. Two years passed and nothing happened. I was earning well. Life as Alphalion seemed good. Then you came. Courtesy the stupidity of Ankit Malik. He approached street peddlers like KD to become seller on Indiparadise.

"I thought to remove you from my way, and I instructed Ankit Malik as Alphalion to handle you. When he failed, I knew you are a tough nut to crack. And an idea sparked in my mind. I thought I could use you to destroy Indiparadise. Tanwar got Karan Shukla killed. The next in line was Ankit Malik. I threatened Ankit Malik to hide in my hideout in Manesar and operate as Alphalion until everything calms down. It was then I who carried out Vishwas Puri's sting operation. And then I sent Indiparadise envelope to Ankit Malik's home where Sabrina was living. I framed Ankit Malik." He winced. "But, Rashmi Purohit, you're truly a tough nut."

Rashmi absorbed Adi's story. It became difficult for her to label Adi with right or wrong. He was only an eighteen year old kid when everything began. May be less. He was over a barrel. And then his employer was killed by her husband. All the more reason for him to comply with Tanwar. But then he continued as Alphalion, he began to enjoy his life as Alphalion. He had power and he had money. His friend was tormented for years before him and he did nothing. "Now that Indiparadise gone," Rashmi said after a brief pause, "do you think Tanwar would forget about you?"

Adi's face leaked no reaction, but his hands grabbing the iron railing were trembling.

Rashmi turned and faced Adi. "Surrender. Go the cops. That's the best shot you've right now. Tell them everything. There will be investigations. There will be trials. I trust on our legal system. And I hope we see Tanwar behind the bars soon."

Chapter 87

Brajesh Arya threw the quarterly get-together a month and a half earlier. His employees thought that it was due to the fact that they'd achieved the target well before the deadline. The truth, however, was that his son was finally happy. Alphalion was behind the bars, the video had been destroyed by the digital forensic experts, and Rohan had successfully appeared for all the exams, and hopefully pass them, too.

Most of the managers from senior management had left. The remaining had occupied the dance floor with their team, their limbs shaking awkwardly like puppets. He considered bidding his employees goodnight and calling it a day. He shot a quick glance toward his secretary, Pooja, to check on her condition. Pooja was raising a toast of tequila shot. It was her fifth of the evening. As she drowned it, she stumbled back and a couple of guys got in action to prevent her from tripping over.

Brajesh pinched his forehead skin. He would've to leave her home today too.

He took a corner seat and pulled out his mobile phone. A news app notification was hanging at the top of the screen.

"Online Drug case takes a U-turn."

He tapped on the screen and the news article filled the screen. He read that a college student named Adi Luthra had appeared before the police, claiming himself to be the Alphalion. *Adi Luthra? Rohan's friend.* The deafening music beats seemed to hammer the revelation into his brain. Adi Luthra, he read further, also revealed that Rishi Tanwar, and not his wife, was the mastermind behind Indiparadise.

There was still no mention of Pi Agency, but Brajesh Arya knew that behind these turn of events was Rashmi Purohit.

Chapter 88

"Any new case?" Akshay asked. He and Diksha returned to office after a paid leave of two days. "We haven't taken any new cases in the past few months, thanks to Brijesh Arya."

"No need to come here tomorrow," Rashmi said. "I am closing this office."

"What?" Diksha squealed, her mouth half open. Her head eyes several times between Rashmi and Akshay.

Rashmi offered an expressionless face. "You have heard it right. I am closing this office."

Akhshay gulped, while Diksha bit her lips.

"Because I am moving this office to Gurgaon," Rashmi said, and cracked up. "Oh, come on, even I can joke sometimes."

"I almost had a stroke," Akshay said, placing his hand on his chest.

"But how?" Diksha asked.

"What do you mean, how? You guys used to often complain that we should make our office a bit more professional."

"Yeah, and we also remember how you used to reprimand us for asking it," Diksha complained.

Rashmi laughed. "Actually, Mr. Arya has gifted us with an office space in his own building."

"Wow! That's great," Akshay said.

"He came to know from my uncle about how we found Alphalion's older posts, and how I got his email ID extracted with the help of my estranged mother." She paused. Her mind started pulling her back to the memories of the past. *Memories are like leeches. And memories are like quick sand.* "Brajesh Arya said that no other detective would've gone to such length for this case. Offering an office space is the least he could do."

"That's so nice of him," Diksha said.

"Actually he gifted it only for the first year. After that, we need to pay for the rent. But I think it's a good deal."

"We're happy to move, in any case," Diksha said.

"And there is more news for you," Rashmi said. "I am moving to Gurgaon as well."

"Are you leaving this house?" Akshay's eyebrows rose.

"Yes. I've decided to move on," Rashmi mused, looking at the wall of photographs. "I mean I decided to move to Gurgaon, as commuting from here every day will be hectic."

Akshay and Diksha nodded in agreement.

"I think I should shift to Gurgaon, too," Akshay said. "I have already seen the traffic on the Mehrauli-Gurgaon road after office hours." He looked at Diksha, sticking out his tongue. "I don't think you'll be there every time to carry me through the metro."

*

"Guys, I am moving to Gurgaon," Akshay told his friends on the WhatsApp group. "Now we can meet more often."

"Great news," wrote one friend.

"Brilliant," wrote another. "So you left that small-time detective job."

"Nope," Akshay replied. "I am still a detective."

"Oh! That's great. Even I dream of being a detective one day."

People are so fake, Akshay thought.

He closed his eyes and remembered Smriti. He checked her profile yesterday. She had checked in at a PVR in Gurgaon with his new boyfriend. His mood had turned sour since then. He thought to ask Diksha to go out for coffee, may be for a movie as well. It had required some great deal of will power to stop himself of texting her.

He feared he was falling for Diksha slowly. He just couldn't stop himself from feeling that way for her. With Smriti, he didn't know that he would end up getting hurt, but with Diksha he knew very well that what the end would be. He knew that Diksha wasn't interested in him and, eventually, would leave him. Yet there was a voice constantly screaming inside his head to tell Diksha that he loved her.

Epilogue

The moving crew packed all the small items first. They started with the utensils, then the books. When they reached for the photo frames, she stopped them. "Leave them for the end," she said.

They then moved to the heavy items. Bed, bookshelf, coffee table, refrigerator, microwave, air-conditioner. In no time, all the household items were stacked on the truck. Now she was left alone inside her house with the Wall of Memories.

She had never seen her house vacant. It looked weird, and it was disheartening to leave the house in which her father had spent his entire life, and in which she was born and brought up. It was this very place where she'd seen all the highs and lows of her life until now.

The Wall of Memories was going to become a memory, too. She had clung enough to this wall, and to the memories, so much so that the memories had become fetters. She doubted whether she was doing the right thing. It felt like she was abandoning her father, just like her mother. Her estranged mother had come to meet her yesterday. Rashmi was not as furious to see her ex-mother this time. After all, Madhu had helped her to find the real Alphalion. But that was not the reason. It was something else. Perhaps she was moving on.

The blank walls, the vacant floors, the echoes, all stared back at her, appeared as if they were sobbing. Her heart wrenched with guilt.

"Ma'am," the mover said, "shall I pack these photographs now?"

She realised he had asked this question for the second time while she was pondering. "Sure," she said, and stepped back. It felt like her ankles were tied to heavy leg irons. *Move on.* The words rang inside her head in her father's voice.

Her father stared right into her eyes, smiling from outside, broken from inside.

She felt like stopping everything right there. Unload everything from the truck and put them back.

The crew member removed the first photo frame, wrapped it under an air bubble sheet and placed it inside a carton. She turned her face away. It was the first time this photo frame was removed from its place since it was hung there. *Move on.*

Emotions whirled inside her like a flooding river. She let out a long and voluminous sigh. She turned and walked out of her house for the last time, recalling something her father had said in the letter. *Move on— two words, an order that must be followed, but which requires you to turn to stone from inside.*